FIST FULL OF PLIGHT

Jamaal Nelson

Chapter One

Lands

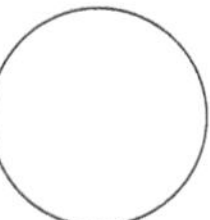

A variation of noises saturated the area. Men talked amongst each other as they stood posted up by their cars, women danced and twerked as their friends' recorded videos, and cars blasted bass-filled music through their speakers while arriving at or parked at the scene. What seemed like an endless aroma of weed stained the air as the crowd smoked blunts freely. The age range of the festive spectators varied drastically. Some were barely old enough to buy a ticket for an R-rated movie, and some neared their ten-year high school reunion. I guarantee summer nights like these bring vibrant energy, rhythm, and excitement. You know, the type only Black people can elicit. I feel these are the golden days older people are always telling young folks like us to enjoy.

My name is Joel, but it's not pronounced like most people would think. It's pronounced *Jole,* not *Joe-el*. This particular car meet, or some say car show, took place in the parking lot of a rundown shopping mall on the east side of the city. Car meets spring up randomly across the city of Indianapolis; also referred to as Naptown or simply Nap for short. If you are connected enough with the right people, you get the word about them through text messages. Along with any other happenings. Like in Fall, I always got word about low-priced Nike sweatsuits from boosters across Nap. Doing any kind of business with a booster is hit or miss. The items could either be named brands or knockoff versions, but you couldn't even tell the difference. Car meets almost always end up being posted and talked about on social media. Instagram, TikTok, Twitter, Facebook, etc. I don't think it's wise to post the details online. 12 can easily look online, pinpoint the time and location, and shut it down. They have many times in the past and will continue to do so in the future. You know the police hate seeing Black folks having a good time. Police, 12, po-po, cops, five-o, pigs, whatever you want to call them. It's all the same. Each car meet kicks off in the evening or later hours of the day. They end whenever people get tired or when 12 pulls up. SRT Chargers, Hellcats, Track Hawks, Camaros, customized old-school whips, and other flashy vehicles stir excitement amongst the roaring spectators as they perform donuts, make sharp uneasy turns, and generate smoke from their tires. Burnt rubber could be smelled from miles away. A good number of them also had 5% tints, with some having 1%. You know; the really dark windows you can easily see through from the inside of the car but see nothing but a dark abyss when looking from the outside. Car meets are filled with predominantly Black spectators and drivers. All rocking overpriced shoes, fresh outfits, haircuts, fresh nails, and a pistol to top everything off. There were more guns than cars in attendance. You don't have to be a so-called street or hood nigga to carry a gun. That's just how the world is today. You never know what could happen, so always have a proper means of protection. Indiana just made a new state law saying we don't even need a permit anymore to carry a pistol. That's sweet music to a lot of Indianapolis native's ears.

"Mu'fuckas been stepping on my shit all night!" Ta'Juan said, referring to the minor scuff to his Jordan Cherry 11's. He lightly licked his thumb to lean over and rubbed the scuff off the toe of his right shoe. He stood posted in front of my grey 2001 Impala. He stood in the middle, Rolan stood to his left, and I stood to his right. We bore witness to the extravagant cars and unpredictable chain of events. I laughed and then responded to Ta'Juan. "Why did you think it was a good idea to wear white shoes to a car meet? You knew it was gone be hella' people here." Rolan smirked as he leaned up against my car with his arms folded. Suddenly, a Black 1999 gloss-painted Cutlass cruised by us. We became fixated on its perfection. The 24-inch rims complemented its elegance. The chopped and screwed version of rapper Pimp C's "Pimpin' Aint' No Illusion" blasted through its trunk rattling speakers. On the other hand, my car is on its last leg with almost every maintenance light on. From the low tire pressure indicator to the engine light. But as long as it keeps getting me from point A to point B, I'm not complaining. I paid $750 for it so I knew what I was getting myself into. The mirror on the passenger side is held together by duct tape. Something in me refuses to come off $65 for a new one. My car speakers are barely functional. They only work on the right passenger side of the car. Ta'Juan usually puts his portable Bluetooth JBL speaker on the dashboard, and we roll with that.

Of the three of us in our dynamic trio, Ta'Juan causes most of the havoc. Once, he called me 'Jewel' instead of Joel, because of my taste in music. I rarely listen to Hip Hop and Rap to get my day started. I like Hip Hop and Rap, but I don't listen to it 24/7 as Ta'Juan does. For example, if it's 7 A.M. I'll be listening to R&B. Ta'Juan will be listening to NBA Youngboy or EST Gee. He thinks listening to R&B is for women or "soft" men. To him, R&B is more depressing than soothing and relaxing. We don't see eye to eye on everything, but we remain solid friends. We always had each other's backs, right or wrong; same with Rolan.

A thin, medium-height man in a Gucci sweatsuit walked by us. His sweatsuit was a few sizes too small for him as the bottom of his jacket rose above his waist and arm sleeves were above his wrists. Possibly to show off his designer underwear and flashy watch. You could see his sweat leaking through his armpits and pouring down his face and neck. I think wearing a sweatsuit in 90-degree weather is crazy, but that's just me. You know some people will go above and beyond just to show off their materialist possessions. He was on the phone yelling something about going to the club after the car meet. He had a pistol, with no gun holster, hanging out in his right pocket. I peeped he had a switch and an extended clip as well. I never saw anything wrong with having protection. Especially for Black people. When you see a white man teaching his five-year-old son how to handle, clean, and shoot a hunting rifle they are not labeled thugs or ghetto, but they label Black people "thugs" and tell us to "put down the guns" even as adults. When you see white individuals shooting up schools and large gatherings of people, why are they not labeled thugs? White people beat that case by being labeled as having a clinical or mental disorder. As if they are the only ones with mental health issues. They get taken into custody while unarmed Black men and women are slaughtered on the scene. For white folks, it's clinical, but for Black folks, it's criminal. Read that again. For instance, take the case of white supremacist Dylann Roof. He walked into a Black church with a rifle killing nine worshipers. What did local law enforcement do after they apprehended him? They treated him to a bite to eat at Burger King. The news and media outlets went above and beyond to paint him as a mental health case rather than a racist white supremacist. George Zimmerman killed an unarmed sixteen-year-old Trayvon Martin and was acquitted even with outstanding evidence indicating his racial hatred. They blame gun violence in Black neighborhoods and communities on everything and everyone except for the initial causes of factors that make a person inevitably respond to their predicament. Poverty, disproportionate distribution of resources, kindergarten to high school curriculums that aren't suitable or don't directly apply to Black people, menticide, mass incarceration, I could go all day. Would you expect a Jew to happily read student books and other material that glorifies Hitler in a positive and heroic light? So why would you expect Black people to happily learn about George Washington, Ben Franklin, Thomas Jefferson, and other founding fathers of America when they owned and raped African slaves? Ben Franklin wrote key parts of the American Constitution and Declaration of Independence. He wrote eloquently about freedom, liberty, and the pursuit of happiness for all people while having dozens of enslaved Africans under his ruling hand.

You hear nothing about Asian-on-Asian violence, Latino-on-Latino violence, or white-on-white violence, so why do we always hear the Black-on-Black violence narrative throughout the media? It's not because Black people are more violent or commit more crimes than any other racial group, so what else could it be? There is a fundamental difference between Black people killing each other and white folks killing Black people. For example, if Marcus kills Rashad, Marcus is getting arrested in the next 24 hours and does life in jail. If white Police Officer Smithers kills unarmed Ja'Darius, he doesn't even get questioned or brought into custody for another week or two. Then, gets paid leave of absence, a book deal, and probably won't even be prosecuted.

For the last few minutes, it was difficult to focus on the cars, because the ladies were looking good. Edges laid, bodies to perfection in their sun dresses, biker shorts, and other revealing clothes to flaunt everything they were born with. Ta'Juan had his eyes set on a girl he thought was eyeing him. "She been eyeing me all night," he said as he continued to look at her from a distance. Rolan and I immediately looked at each other and smirked. We were all still posted by my Impala. I responded, "Nah bro, I think she was just looking at the cars passing by. Just like we were." Rolan laughed. "Ight, we gone see about that," Ta'Juan said with a slight grin. He began to slowly make his way over in her direction. She stood by a silver Nissan Altima wearing a gold necklace around her neck with a pendant that reads "*Tierra*" hanging from it. Tierra was accompanied by two other Black girls who looked to be her friends. Tierra was dark-skinned with long flowing locs. Her skin radiated with melanin in the kind moonlight. She was no taller than 5'2. Real petite figure. Her friend standing to her left was a tall, brown-skinned beauty. She had to be 5'9 or 5'10. She had piercings all over her entire right ear, belly, lip, and nose. You could see her nipple piercings through her shirt. Nothing clung to her left ear. The other friend to her right was brown-skinned and the same height as Tierra. She rocked pink box braids and a hoop piercing on her nose. When Ta'Juan finally approached Tierra, he didn't sound as smooth as he thought he did. "Aye, how you what?" he said. The term how you what is local Indianapolis slang for a variety of things. Depending on how it's used, it can mean what's going on, what are you trying to do, or sometimes can mean to agree with something or someone but in this particular situation Ta'Juan meant it as what are you trying to do. Ta'Juan went on, "You been looking good all night. You gone keep staring at me or give me your number?" Rolan and I stood twenty feet away bearing witness. We couldn't hear a single word being said, but the reaction from Tierra and her friends told us everything we needed to know. The three of them shot one another a look with their mouths dropped open. They simultaneously laughed right in Ta'Juan's face. After 5 long seconds of laughter passed, Tierra finally responded. "Boy, ain't nobody checking for your dusty ass." Ta'Juan just stood there, not quite knowing how to respond and a little caught off-guard. I'm sure she was accustomed to being approached by egotistic men all the time, but not quite how Ta'Juan just had. She added, "Plus my boyfriend around here somewhere looking for me." That might have been true, but sometimes females say that when they don't want to talk to you. In my opinion, it's best for guys to take the hints females throw at them and charge it to the game. Take the "L" (a loss, to lose, or not accomplish something) and move on. There are more women you can try your chances on. Plenty more fish in the sea. After the flop of an attempt to get a girl, Ta'Juan took his "L" to the chin and headed back towards Rolan and me. We were both dying of laughter. It was 11 P.M. as the night sky hosted the moon and a steaming summer heat.

Suddenly, an all-black SRT Charger pulled up a few feet away from Tierra and her friends. A dark-skinned man wearing a black t-shirt, light blue skinny jeans with a tan Gucci belt with green and red trim, and black Balenciaga shoes hopped out of the car. His face was engulfed with rage. Rapper NBA YoungBoy's song "Green Dot" blasted from his car. He bullied the driver's door open. His tight-fitting t-shirt gave away the bulge on his right hip, indicating he had some type of hidden weapon. Another man wearing a white shirt also stood only a few feet away from where Tierra and her friends stood. He backs his back towards the girls as he was taking a phone call. His phone call was abruptly cut short, with his phone flying out of his hands. The man in black ran up and swung at the man in white. He snuck him. His body smacked the ground. He never saw it coming. Multiple bystanders could be heard. "Daaamn!" and "Ahh shit!" Or even a long exaggerated "Oooh!" A few hours later I found out on Instagram that the fight broke out because the man in white was on Twitter talking crazy. He said something disrespectful about the other man's friend that got killed. He tweeted, "That nigga P-lo always been pussy. May he rest in piss." No more than fifteen minutes later, there was a second fight between two females. One of the females who fought was Tierra, who claimed she had a boyfriend. The funny thing is she fought over a guy that couldn't care less about either one of them. His name is Dre. He's always been known for messing with two or more females at one time, but he's a player about it. He always lets his women know that he entertains more than one woman. Maybe they fought thinking the winner would gain Dre, who knows?

Chapter Two

Day 1

I met Ta'Juan back in middle school; 7th grade to be exact. We both went to East Gate Junior High. Ta'Juan was a new student from another school. He was kicked out of his old school while notorious for fighting classmates and verbally attacking his teachers. Eventually, he got expelled. East Gate was willing to accept him for enrollment just a few weeks before winter break began.

I remember it being a frosty winter morning when I was walking to my bus stop. It was at the entrance to the apartment complex we lived in. There was a light layer of snow on the ground, causing limited traction for walking. It didn't help that there was also ice on the sidewalks and roads. I rode bus #20. My bus arrived a few minutes late. Ms. Perkins, my bus driver, normally arrived at 7:20 A.M. but was ten minutes later than usual that day. I knew because I had a red watch my mom got me for my birthday that year. The screech from the brakes screamed until the bus came to a complete standstill. The bus door slid open. I got on and walked, headed to my seat. The frost from the winter elements stained each window on the bus. Some of the kids would use their fingers to trace all types of finger art. A girl named Devia got kicked off the bus for tracing the word "Bitch!" with a smiley face underneath on a window in the back. There were two students to a seat, but there was an odd number of kids, so I sat by myself. When I arrived at my seat I figured out why Ms. Perkins was a few minutes late. We had a new student on our bus, so she had to make an extra stop. On Ta'Juan's first day, he was assigned to sit by me. He was sitting by the window. "Wassup bro," I said to him with my hand extended to dap him up. "Wassup, I'm Ta'Juan, but people call me Big Juan," he said with a smile. I responded, "Who calls you that?" I asked, confused. He laughed, "Well, nobody calls me that. I just wanted to have a cool nickname. My real name is Ta'Juan." We both laughed. Every bus ride was nothing but laughs the entire school year.

Winter passed, spring came and went, and it was now deep into the summer festivities. It was the summer right before our first year of high school. Some went to their grandparents for the summer, some got jobs at fast food spots or grocery stores, some played video games 24/7, and some did nothing but be adventurous outside.

Ta'Juan and I always like to hoop at German Church Park. Some of the most talented basketball players on the east side of Nap go there. Some could have easily earned a spot on their school team if their grades and behavior weren't so poor. This particular day was one of the hottest summers on record, according to the local news stations. It was so hot that you could be laying down in bed, eyes closed, and still be visualizing heat waves from earlier. Ta'Juan would always say, "How you gone expect me to act like I got some sense when it's this hot outside?"

The fellas at the park wore white beaters and tanks as sweat from their pores magnified their melanin. It was either that or be shirtless altogether in an attempt to fight off the blazing sun. The blacktop of the basketball court was hot enough to fry an egg. The girls stood on the sidelines wearing different assortments of tops and shorts. Some girls were also waiting to jump in on the next pickup game. None of the boys would admit this, but a few of the girls were better than half the guys. Some of the guys didn't come to hoop. Their agendas were checking the sidelines and other areas of the park to talk to girls. Parents were sitting on the old silver park benches watching their children scream and play as they swung on the swing sets, rode down on the slides, and chased each other through the old brown mulch. There was also a small but heavily used section of the park where water shot up from four small holes beneath the concrete. Children laughed and smiled ear to ear as they ran through the water shooting up into their innocent faces. There was a woman standing a couple of feet away from the swing set. She was on the phone as well as taking breaks from her phone call to yell at her kids. "Damn why yall being so damn loud! Don't get yo ass whooped in front of all these people!" Why would you bring them to the park if you didn't want them to be loud and have fun?

Ta'Juan comes to the park for two reasons and two reasons only. If he's not playing basketball, he sells weed, lean, pills, a known booster, and anything else he can get his hands on. He is also one of the best scammers in the city. He once took a hundred-dollar bill to a bank and flipped it into a thousand dollars. I don't know how he does it. Ta'Juan could have easily landed a starting spot for our school basketball team if it wasn't for his poor grades and behavior. I'm a semi-decent player but just don't have much interest in basketball. I do like trash-talking though. I may not be the next LeBron James, but I love talking trash on the court like Draymond Green. That's one thing I've always been good at and did better than anyone else. I know how to get into my opponent's head and throw them off their game. My dad said I got that trait from him. He was an amazing player. He played high school and college ball right here in the city. He won three state championships at Cardinal Central High School during his sophomore, junior, and senior year as the starting point guard. He was even voted Mr. Basketball during his final year. His very last high school game was one for the record books. This game won his third Indiana state basketball title. His team won by a point due to a missed free throw by the rival team. The rival player had hit the first of two shots with one second left in the game. The rival teams' crowd roared with excitement and applause as they were now down by one point. On the opposite end of the court sat our team's crowd screaming their hearts out while doing any type of distracting taunt in hopes of making the rival player miss his shot. After the first free throw, the ref held the ball, waiting for the rival player to signal he was ready for his final shot. The player took two small steps back, took three slow deep breaths, then slowly returned to the free throw line. Everybody in the stadium noticed how visibly nervous he was. His hands were trembling, eyes wide, and his breaths were short and hasty. He then took another step back. My dad simply walked up behind him. He said three simple words in a cool and collected voice. "You ain't shit," then both walked back to their positions. He finally put up the shot. It hit the left of the rim. A miss for him, but a state title for my dad and his team.

My dad's government name is Kenneth Bernard Jackson, but mostly everybody calls him Kenny. I call him Pops. He once told me I was almost named Kenny Jr, but my parents decided to name me Joel at the last second. He said it came from something they found in the Bible. Pops never cusses. He is a devout Christian. He and my momma made sure I made it to church every Sunday. We sometimes went on Tuesdays for choir rehearsal and Thursdays for Bible study. New Start Fellowship Church was home to us and hundreds of other families across the city. Rolan is a lot like my Pops. Even though he is a Muslim, they share a lot of the same values and mindset. I have never heard Rolan cuss before. Instead, he encourages Ta'Juan and me to "Articulate your words in a way that reflects greatness upon you." Rolan also often quotes the mighty Malcolm X, "A man cusses because he doesn't have the words to say what's on his mind."

Ta'Juan and I met Rolan for the first time on a scorching summer day. Rolan brought his younger brother Stadan with him to the park. Just a few weeks before, they moved to Indianapolis from Accra, Ghana. One of the many countries on the continent of Africa. They both speak two fluent languages. English and Akan. Their dad found a great job in the city which was the reason for their big move across the world. I could see them both standing on the sidelines from the opposite end of the court. They arrived about ten minutes after Ta'Juan and I did. We were waiting on the sideline to play in the next five on five full court pickup game. The winning team keeps playing and the losing team steps off the court. I tapped Ta'Juan on his shoulder to get his attention. "Aye Ta'Juan, who are those two guys standing over there? I've never seen them before," I asked. Ta'Juan looked over in their direction. He responded, "I don't know them niggas," he said, and then re-shifted his focus to the current pickup game. Rolan and Stadan stood out more than anyone at the park. Primarily due to their size and physique. Rolan is tall and muscular. He stands at six feet two inches. Stadan is only a couple of years younger, but tall for his age. He is six feet tall, while Ta'Juan stands at five feet ten inches. I on the other hand have always been a small guy. Even in middle school when everybody was hitting puberty, it seemed like I was the only late bloomer. During those years, most boys my age were fifteen or sixteen years old looking like their twenty-fifth birthday was coming up. I'm only five feet six and a half inches tall but I tell people I'm five foot seven. I like to round it up, especially when I'm talking to a girl I like.

Two players from the winning team stepped off the court after running three games back-to-back. They were both visibly exhausted. That gave Ta'Juan and I the opportunity to fill in since we were up next. Another team of five slowly developed as they were picking their team members. Since the team we joined just won, we got the ball first to start the game. We quickly won two games back-to-back. The blazing heat made our opponents even more frustrated and annoyed when I talked trash to them. I was talking so much trash that opposing players were missing wide-open layups, turning the ball over, and altogether making them look silly. During our first game of the day, I made somebody walk off the court in the middle of the game. He missed two three-point shots in a row. So, it was only right that I said, "You so fucking sorry. Take yo' weak ass home." He tried to act like I wasn't getting to him by responding, "Yeah, ight nigga. Watch me on this next play." But he would end up either missing another wide-open shot then turning the ball over to my team on his next possession. He stormed off the court as everybody heckled and laughed. Shayla, who lives down the street from me, had been waiting on the sideline as well and replaced him. Known her since 4th grade and man she can hoop for real! In the first game, we won 21 to 3. The second game ended with a score of 21 to 9. Ta'Juan had most of the points each game. Well, all of the points in the second game and 12 during our first game. But I had the most assists!

Rolan and Stadan sat on a long silver bench off to the side of the court. They were patiently waiting for the golden moment to show their skills on the blacktop. "Ight who up next?" Ta'Juan yelled as he moved his head from left to right, scanning the sidelines. He was standing in the middle of the court holding the basketball. Rolan and Stadan finally stood up. Two other guys who sat beside them followed suit. "Here I come," another female hooper said as she sat on the sideline, continuing to stretch her right leg. "Bet. Let's run it," Ta'Juan said. Soon, Rolan's team was on the court, standing side by side. Our team received the ball first. Ta'Juan checked the ball in with Rolan, and the game had begun. It seemed like as soon as Rolan and Stadan checked the ball, the new kids on the block proved how much game they had. I guarded Stadan since he was slightly shorter than Rolan. Ta'Juan was 5 feet 10 inches with long arms and legs, so he had the best chance of guarding Rolan. With their playing styles on the court, they favored professional players. Rolan was explosive, aggressive, and dominated the paint like Giannis Antetokounmpo. He would even check the ball like he had every dollar to his name bet on the game. Stadan was a great perimeter scorer and passer like Scottie Pippen. They eventually handed us our first loss of the day. Ta'Juan didn't take the loss well and decided to respond in hostility. "Man, yall really bitch made! Hoe ass niggas lucky I'm tired and didn't really play like I normally do," he said not looking directly at Rolan and Stadan but we all knew who he was talking to. Rolan and Stadan's other team members had already left the court. They were talking amongst each other, posted by their cars in the parking lot behind the playground. Our team was still on the court, but the other members said nothing. Rolan responded, "Brother, it's not that serious. You had a great game. It's all for fun." He stuck his hand out to dap him up. Ta'Juan smacked his lips, "Schhh," and then blew Rolan off. Stadan had kept his cool so far, but you could tell he didn't have much more left. A few spectators laughed. A random guy on the sideline yelled, "Nigga I know you ain't gone let him talk to you like that!" Seemed like everyone on the sideline was either instigating, laughing, or had their phones out to record. Others on the other side of the park quickly sensed the growing tension on the court. Arguments or disagreements could easily lead to a fight, stabbing, shooting, or full-on brawl. Ta'Juan gave a sly smirk. I had the feeling he was about to do something crazy. He looked Rolan dead in his face and calmly said, "I'll beat anybody ass out here." I didn't know if he could beat anybody up at the park, but I did know he wasn't hesitant to at least try. Some of the spectators and families began to leave the park. The people who stayed put wanted to see a fight. Parents were gathering their kids and speed walking, some running, to their cars. Stadan finally responded in defense of his brother, "Rolan is a little more patient and forgiving than I am. Because I will lay yo' weak ass out right now," he said as he and Rolan stood side by side, fists clutched together. Their faces were stern and furious. The brothers stood firmly in anticipation of swinging at any other offense made by Ta'Juan. I understood their feelings of disrespect and slight embarrassment by Ta'Juan's comments. Ta'Juan took a step closer to Stadan and then looked him up and down slowly. Rolan was making him look like a little boy due to his size. "Aye, if niggas tryna' throw down pop off then pussy ass nigga," Ta'Juan said in all seriousness. He then got in a southpaw fighting stance. I've seen his Glock 19 dozens of times. I've been telling him to get rid of the illegal switch modification he has on it but I hadn't seen either all day so I was relieved because you never know what Ta'Juan will do. I knew I'd have to intervene at some point to cool things down.

For some reason, this incident reminded me of a video I saw on TikTok by a guy named Brother Jamaal. He touched on the importance of learning, relating to, and incorporating what you learn about the past into your present to increase your potential to have a better overall quality of life in the future. In one of his videos, he said, "Any problem or issue you have today somebody in the past has gone through it and created a solution to resolve it. All you have to do is not just learn but apply the same methods they did to your present issues, short-coming, or difficulties." He had another video I liked too. He said, "Black or African Americans come from African descent. We may have been born in America, but we are still Africans. The African genotype instilled within us comes with numerous unique qualities and graces. Our rhythm, intelligence, creativity, inventiveness, melanin, etc. Our nationality is American, but we're Africans who have been displaced from the mother lands due to slavery." I googled it but didn't look into it. I also remember my old social studies teacher Mr. Stenson going out of his way to teach us about our true history. "Africa, African history, African American history, and are all the same. Just in different places in the world but the same people," he would say. With our school being 72% Black, it always fascinated me every time he would speak. He'd often get in trouble with our white superintendent Ms. Ross for "failing to comply with the school's curriculum guidelines" which were white or European-focused studies. Eventually, Mr. Stenson was forced to retire. He's currently taking the entire school district to court over the decision. He spoke at our high school graduation right before he was forced into retirement. "We are Africans before we are American. African American means people of African descent who reside in America. Displaced from their native land, culture, morays, folkways, norms, customs, traditions, language, and more. We're still denied the things allotted to Americans. Political control, an economic base, reparations, land, social control, and more."

All eyes were still fixated on the four of us in the middle of the basketball court. I took a glance around and it seemed like even more people than before were now recording on their phones. I finally figured out what to try in hopes of cooling things down. I gave a forced laugh, "Ta'Juan, you funny bro. Aye, he didn't mean no disrespect. He just real competitive. I think it's good y'all gave us our first loss of the day. It challenges us to go harder next time," I said. Rolan, who now had his attention on me, smiled and dapped me up. "I appreciate that bro. What's yo' name?" he asked me. I could tell Rolan is not the type that allows things to bother him easily due to the way he was handling the situation. His younger brother Stadan on the other hand was a different story. "Joel," I responded with a light smile. Ta'Juan spoke, "Yeah, you right. I was just fucking with y'all." That's Ta'Juan's way of giving an apology. Rolan then dapped up Ta'Juan showing acceptance of his apology. Stadan was hesitant at first. He looked at Rolan. Rolan gave him a nod, then Stadan eventually followed suit. "I like the way you diffused this minor conflict brother. You on Instagram? This is the type of conflict resolution I try to teach our people. I'm still trying to teach my brother as well," he said, smiling and giving Stadan an innocent punch on the shoulder. Stadan laughed. Rolan pulled out his phone and I did as well. "Hell yeah, my name is Joelx317," I said. Rolan typed in my name and then hit me with a follow. I immediately noticed he had 11k followers on Instagram. We dapped each other up again, then Ta'Juan and I headed to my car. We stopped at McDonald's for a quick burger and fries before I drove him home. He lives with his baby momma and two kids.

After dropping Ta'Juan off, I randomly decided to contact a longtime friend of mine named D'Marcus. It was 8:15 P.M. at the time. I texted him earlier asking if it would be okay for me to come by. He responded a few minutes later as I sat in my car listening to SIR's new album. He's one of my favorite R&B artistes of this generation. "My nigga! You know my momma been saying you're welcome whenever you want to come by." D'Marcus and I have been tight for a minute. Years before I met Ta'Juan or Rolan. I was in 3rd grade while D'Marcus was in 2nd. We went to school together from elementary school to my 8th-grade year. That's when D'Marcus' mom transferred him to a fancy prep school called Ronald Reagan Academy. It's for the so-called "gifted and talented" students in the most suburban city in Indiana called Carmil. Aside from having the most roundabouts in the country, Carmil, Indiana is also home to some of the most racist residents in the state. Many of them were supporters of Donald Trump. It was no surprise after the storming of the US Capitol building, people soon figured out twenty-six Carmil residents were caught participating. Local doctors, policemen, educators, and other Carmil residents with important positions of power were amongst the ones caught. There were probably more of them, but only twenty-six of them were identified. D'Marcus called me one night with all the details. "Yeah, my biology teacher Mr. Jones got caught at the storming of the capital building. His face was on the news and everything. We were in the middle of class while he was teaching when I first saw the picture of him on social media. He didn't know until a student raised her hand, showed a picture of him from her phone to the class, and asked if the picture was really of him." I still get upset about how he changed schools, but I understand his mom just wants the best for him. It's a parent thing. If I'm ever blessed to have kids, I'm giving them everything I didn't have growing up. Give them a head start in life. My parents did an amazing job raising me, but they struggled financially, physically, emotionally, and mentally, and are still struggling today. They are not in a position to give me a start in life or pass anything down to me. They thought working hard at their jobs was the solution, but they are still working non-stop with almost nothing to show for it. Like when I turned 18, everything was all on me. It's interesting how other groups like whites and Hispanics allow their sons and daughters to live with them until their late twenties or early thirties with no contest. They save up so much money by doing so, but most Black households want you out and on your own by 18. Still a teenager. How can a parent possibly expect their son or daughter to be successful if you are forcing them to take on the world all by themselves as a teenager?

I finally got to D'Marcus' house. I texted him, "I'm pulling up" when I was two minutes away as a heads up. I hadn't been over since my high school graduation. A little over a year ago. I used to come over almost every weekend back in middle school. He's a high school senior year now. D'Marcus stays with his mom due to his dad never being in the picture. He never even brings up his dad in conversation.

The outside of their house needs some work done, but it's a true site to see on the inside. His mom could be an interior designer if she wanted. She always switches up their home décor. For example, you could walk in one day to a red color scheme. Different shades of red and reddish patterns from the couch, window drapes, rug, lamp, art on the wall, and more. Another possibility could be different animal prints displayed. You just never know what kind of creative assortments she will come up with. After parking, I walked up and stood on their porch steps. Their driveaway is a mixture of rocks and grass in front of their house. Their porch was small, with tiny narrow cement steps leading up to the front door. It was late at night, so I didn't want to ring the doorbell or knock on the door too hard, sounding like the police. I texted D'Marcus to let him know I was outside. Moments later, I heard two or three different locks being opened from the inside. Finally, D'Marcus swung the door open and greeted me with a warm smile. "Wassup G! Man, it's been a minute. I can't even remember the last time I saw you in person!" D'Marcus said with boisterous excitement. I returned the smile, matching his energy. "Yeah, it's been a long time for real!" I said. "Come in bro, but take your shoes off at the door," D'Marcus said as he held the door open for me to enter. I crept in. After I was inside, D'Marcus peeped his head out of the front door behind me. He took a quick look around outside, then pulled his head back into the house, closing the door. The first thing I noticed about the inside was the elegance of the home setup. To the right sat a leather navy blue couch with one light blue fur pillow to the left of the couch and one regular blue fur pillow to the right. The couch sat in front of the living room window. Their 70-inch TV looked even more massive due to how small their living room is. It sat mounted to the wall about twenty feet across from the couch. The small hallway and entry to the two bedrooms was to the left of the TV. The window curtains added to the aesthetic. Navy blue with sparkling crystals alongside the trim of the curtains. There was a fish tank with a silver casing sitting directly below the TV. I especially liked the fur rug flat in the middle of the living room. It was a mixture of regular blue, navy blue, and light blue. The entry to the kitchen was to the right of the TV. The kitchen is rather small but still nice. There sat a small circular-shaped table with two chairs on one side of the kitchen with the stove, microwave above it, and other kitchen essentials directly across from it. On the table, lay a navy-blue cloth on it and stood a few feet to the right of the couch.

D'Marcus' mother was sitting on the couch in her relaxation attire which consisted of a black bonnet, a throwback 1993 Indy Black Expo shirt that was a couple of sizes too big, and some grey Nike sweatpants. She looked a bit tired as if she just got off from a long shift at work. She greeted me, "Hey sweetie, how you been doing?" she asked with a loving grin. You could tell she was trying her best to be polite even though she was tired, but still happy to see me. I responded, "I'm good ma'am. Just been working." She then asked how my mom was doing. I had to take a step back and remind myself she and my mom had been best friends throughout high school. Never thought to ask why they stopped. I responded to her, "She's doing good ma'am. I'll let her know you asked about her." Her sly grin then turned into a full-blown smile. "There you go being all polite as usual. You know you can just call me Jessica sweetie," she said. I smiled with confirmation.

After the small chat with Jessica, D'Marcus' and I walked down the hallway leading into his room. The hallway, though small, had walls containing a few pieces of beautiful paintings and photos. On the left side was a selection of paintings by local Black Indianapolis artists. D'Marcus' mother made it a habit to ask the artist their selling price for their artwork, then add on an additional $50. To the right hung photographs of a D'Marcus as a baby and his elementary school years, along with a framed picture of many pivotal Black leaders and scholars' faces. Martin Luther King Jr. Assata Shakur, Malcolm X, Barrack Obama, Betty Shabazz, Angela Davis, Khallid Muhammad, Marcus Garvey, and more. I thought to myself, with D'Marcus mother being so invested in supporting the local Black talents, and the Black community, and remembering pivotal Black figures, why did she move her son from a predominately Black school to a predominately white school?

We entered D'Marcus' room. I sat down on his futon while he sat on his bed. I immediately noticed two packs of Backwoods next to his pillow. "Nigga, put that up before yo' momma see it," I whispered. He laughed, "Bro, you know what's crazy? She don't even care no more. All them years of her being against weed, now she smokes," he said. I was stunned because I remember her kicking an old boyfriend of hers out of the house when I came over a few years ago. All because he smelled like weed.

D'Marcus began telling me about a few experiences at his prep school. He's the only person I know personally that goes to a prep school. I was now lying on my back on his black futon, tossing a small NERF basketball in the air. "It's some white folks that stay in their lane and culture. They don't do no extra shit. Then you got the ones that try to act Black. Dress like us, listen to our music, use our lingo and slang but butcher the fuck out of it," we both laughed. He continued, "Heard a white girl the other day get her test back in Math after our teacher graded it. I'm guessing she got a good grade cause' when she looked at her test she said, 'yeah per-riod' instead of just period like Black girls be saying." We both laughed again. He continued, "Then one time, it was a free day in the gym, so the substitute teacher didn't care what we did as long as we stayed in the gym. Some people were chillin' cracking jokes, some making Tik Toks, some listening to music on the bleachers, whatever. You know how them substitute teachers be cool as fuck. So,

I was chillin' on the bleachers looking through Instagram and listening to music with my headphones." He picked up a half drank water bottle from the dresser by his bed. Took a sip and then continued, "Out of nowhere, I felt a tap on my shoulder, so I took one headphone out. It was one of the white boys saying I could be team captain if I wanted to. I'm sitting there confused. So, I asked the team captain of what? He laughed and said the captain for the pickup game they were about to start. Then he pointed over in the direction of one of the basketball goals. It was like ten white boys and one nigga smiling and waving in my direction. Coon ass nigga. What made them automatically assume I can hoop? I can't even think about dribbling a basketball without losing my concentration." They both started laughing again. I noticed on the other side of his bed a stack of paper. "What's them papers over there?" I asked. "It's this article I printed off the internet about why Martin Luther King Jr. ended up agreeing with Malcolm X towards the end of his life."

I graduated high school a year ago, but it feels like it's been a lot longer. I still don't have the slightest idea of what I want to do but I do know what I don't want to do if that makes sense. I'm not tryna' be slaving away at a dead-end job. Many of my family members have been clocking in forty-plus hours a week for decades just to bring home a paycheck that barely keeps enough gas in their car or food on the table. They have almost nothing to show for all those years of hard work they put in. Breaking their backs for minimum wage or $15 an hour, which is nothing nowadays.

Depression has been a constant visitor. Seems like everybody I see on social media has their life planned out and is doing well for themselves. Then there's me. I feel like I'm not doing enough. I have just been working a bullshit job. I mean it's coo' for now but it's not going to get me anywhere in the future. I work at a shoe store called Vick's. I have been there since my sophomore year of high school. I have always been a shoe fanatic. Jordans, Nikes, Adidas, Pumas, New Balance, you name it. I don't trip about the brand; I cop shoes by how they look. I got the job thanks to my man Keshawn. Keshawn had been working at Vick's a few months before I got hired, so he referred me. I remember meeting my manager Rey and he said as long as I come to work on time, I'll always have a job. Sadly, Keshawn got killed just a few days after my first week. Keshawn got into an argument with his baby momma's boyfriend at Doc's Corner store. It resulted in the baby daddy pulling out a gun. All Vick's employees receive a 40% discount off any of the shoes and 20% off clothing at the store. I share it with my friends and family. Rolan isn't too hyped over shoes, but Ta'Juan is. He's always asking me about the latest Jordans and Nike Dunk releases. He doesn't like using apps because he never hits on shoe raffles. He also never hits on the bets he places on sporting apps, but he keeps going for some reason.

Winter came and was going by fast. I went to work on a Sunday morning at 11 A.M. and got off work at 6 P.M. On Sundays, we close earlier than our normal closing time, which is 8 P.M. Had a pretty busy day. Mainly had a lot of shoe returns and exchanges since it was the week after Christmas. I was planning to play NBA 2K on my PlayStation when I got home. Ta'Juan had been texting in our group chat with him, Rolan, and me about how good the new update is. I was scheduled to be closing the store by myself that night. I have been closing so often at Vick's that my tasks have become second nature. I often play music with my headphones in as I close up. Count the cash in the register, make sure all the merchandise on display is neat, sweep and mop, then lock up the two entry points to the store. The back entrance is for employees, deliveries, and taking out the trash. As soon as you walk out the back door, you'll see a dumpster and an open parking lot for mall employees. The front and main entrance to Vick's connects to the inside of the mall for customers. Customers either come through two large glass doors or window shop as they gaze at the stylish collection of shoes and apparel. From inside the store, I let down the security gate as part of the closing process. It comes down the outside of the glass doors so no one can break through. I lock the gate, then lock the glass entry doors as a second measure of security. You need a special key for the security of both. I make sure both keys stay on one big key ring, so they don't get lost. After I was done closing, I headed for the back door to leave. After 8 P.M. the backdoor automatically locks by itself once it closes.

I headed to my car fighting through the brutal winter elements. I had on a black Nike sweatsuit, gloves, and a black winter hat. It was extremely windy that night. I got a few notifications on my phone from the iPhone weather app indicating severe winds up to 15 mph. It being 12 degrees outside made it feel even worse against my skin. I remember being relieved the parking lot was empty. That meant nobody would have to hear me starting my car. My engine is louder than those unexpected amber alerts you get on your phone. I was almost at my car when I heard a voice yelling out from the shadows. My initial thought was I forgot to close the music app on my phone. The voice was getting louder but I was still confused about what or whom the noise was coming from. It didn't help that the wind was gradually blowing stronger and attacking my ears. I got to my car. As soon as I was about to open the driver's side door, I saw something slowly approaching my direction. It was hard to see due to both the dark evening hours and the dim parking lot light limiting my visibility. "Hey, didn't you hear me calling for you?" a feminine voice yelled. She was now no more than two feet away from me. The night, strong wind gusts, and her hood over her face in an attempt to fight off the brutal wind, made it impossible for me to see her face. She also wore a purple coat that covered her entire body from the hood on her head to her ankles. I responded confused as to what she was talking about. "My fault, do I know you?" I asked. That was all I could manage to get out of my mouth. "No, but I think you may need this." She handed me my wallet. She then continued, "You dropped it when you were walking out of your store. I was walking out my store's back entrance when I saw it on the ground. You were the only other person out here, so I knew it had to be yours. It's too cold for you to be dropping things and then having me chase you down." "I appreciate it," I responded. The lights in the parking lot began to flicker on and off. She then turned around and walked off. I asked for her name but got no response. I guess the wind could be blamed for her possibly not hearing me.

I hopped in my car and immediately cut the heat on. "Shit" was all I could manage to say in response to how brutally cold it was. I hooked up the aux cord to my iPhone. My car is too old for Bluetooth. During my lunch break, I saw Lurk Durk dropped a new song with Lil Baby after checking my Instagram. D'Marcus texted me earlier about Babyface Ray, Larry June, and Rod Wave also dropped some new music. My top five rappers of all time are Kendrick Lamar, Gucci Mane, Rick Ross, Kanye West, and Young Dolph. But my love for rap/hip-hop is nothing compared to my love for R&B. Ari Lennox, SZA, Brent Faiyaz, Summer Walker, H.E.R., Jhene Aiko, and a few others. Old-school R&B, especially the 90's era, is my favorite. I like the early 2000's joints too. Keith Sweat, Anthony Hamilton, Boyz II Men, Jodeci, Tony! Toni Tone, Maxwell, Mary J Blidge, Anita Baker, DeAngelo, Lauryn Hill, Musiq, Fantasia, Erykah Badu, Jill Scott, Ashanti, the list is endless! There are so many R&B artists I listen to that it's impossible to name all of them. My favorite songs of all time are *International Players Anthem* by UGK [Bun B and Pimp C] featuring Outkast [Big Boi and Andre 3000] and Michael Jackson's *Got To Be There* and *The Lady In My Life.* Right before I was about to play Youngboy's new album, I got a call from my momma. She was asking if I'm coming over for dinner. She was going to make me a plate if I was. "Hey momma, nah I'm not gone be able to swing by tonight. I'll come by sometime this week tho'. Love you," I said. I moved out of my parent's crib a few months after I graduated high school. It's almost as if my parents give me more attention now that I'm out of the house than when I lived with them. I love my parents, but I couldn't stand living under their roof. Too many rules. Have to be in the house before 8 P.M., couldn't smoke, church on Sundays and Thursdays, no loud music, chores, don't park in the driveway, the list goes on. When I was younger, I would get whooped for almost anything. I once got whooped for asking why I get whooped so often. Rolan once told me his objections to whooping a child. "You are striking a child with a belt to teach them what? Kids are often too young to understand what they're getting whooped for. You're teaching them that it's okay to resort to violence when you are disappointed or mad at someone. That causes anger and resentment which people tend to take it out on each other rather than the person causing the pain. That's what the white slave master did to the enslaved Africans or Black people."

I believe in God, but never really understood the Bible or Christianity. I'm not against it, I'm just confused. Not just Christianity but religion as a whole has confused me my entire life. Ta'Juan doesn't believe in anything, but Rolan is a devout Muslim. He grew up in a Muslim household. In Sunday school, they taught us that the father, the son, and Holy Spirit are what make up God. That is a mathematical irregularity. Three of anything can't evenly make up a whole. 100% doesn't equally divide into three. One whole fraction can't be broken up into three equal parts. Why do Christians celebrate Christianity when it's not mentioned once in the Bible? How do Muslims know that the Quran is 100% authentic and is the true word of God?

I hopped onto the highway and headed to my 1-bedroom apartment. When driving by my apartment complex, it's impossible not to notice it. The outside of the apartment building is a dark, reddish-like color, which makes the entire apartment complex stick out like a sore thumb. The speed limit is fifty-five miles per hour, but I always push at least seventy miles per hour. I finally arrived at my apartment. I hopped out of my car and headed to my unit. I lived in one of the buildings where you walk through a door and there are different living units from A-F. I lived in unit E which is a walk up one flight of stairs to get to. I only had one neighbor across the hall who lived in unit F. Everybody else stayed downstairs on the first floor. The cold weather already had me annoyed so this note on the door magnified my irritation. I ripped it off my door and began to read. It wasn't the first-time apartment management slapped a note on my door due to my neighbor snitching or complaining about something. They posted a note last month due to "an anonymous complaint from a resident" about my music being too loud. The note was from the apartment complex yet again warning me to stop smoking weed in my apartment. I balled up the note and threw it across the hall toward my neighbor's door. I knew it was his bitch ass. He knocked on my door last week talking about I need to park straight into the spaces. I responded, "It's my parking spot for my unit so I can park however I want as long as I am not in the way of any else's car. Get the fuck away from me." He was always snitching and by himself. 50 years old and doesn't know how to mind his own business.

I finally walked into my apartment, locked the front door, and headed straight to my room. Before I could even take my shoes off my phone started to ring. "Hello?" I answered. It wasn't a saved contact in my phone, so I didn't know who was calling. "Aye Joel, it's De'Ante. This my new number," he said. De'Ante is one of my co-workers at Vick's. I responded, "Wassup bro. Imma' hit you back. I just got off and am about to go to sleep," De'Ante responded, "Hold up real quick bro. Have you been on Twitter?" I was sitting on my bed taking my shoes and socks off. I was so tired and didn't feel like talking but I managed to respond. "Nah bro, I ain't been on Twitter since this morning. I'm just now getting to the crib." De'Ante continued, "Some niggas just robbed a few stores in the mall," he said. My heart sunk deep into my chest. My initial thought was if I remembered to lock up the front entrance to the store. My phone buzzed as I was on the phone with De'Ante. It was a text from Rolan of a speech by Kwame Ture he's been wanting me to listen to. I ignored Rolan's text for the time being. De'Ante abruptly hung up. He dropped his phone in water the other day so it often hangs up his calls and other random stuff. He then shot me a text saying Rey was going to check the security cameras tomorrow to see if the robbers came in through Vick's back or front entrance.

For the next few hours, all I saw on Instagram and Twitter were pictures and videos of how the robbers ransacked and damaged the stores in the mall. Footlocker, Vicks, Victoria's Secret, H&M, Claires, Target, and a few others. We didn't even have any new shoes in the store. All we had were mainly Nike Air Force Ones and shoes that have been on display for about two weeks that nobody will ever buy. We weren't expecting a shipment until tomorrow for the new Jordans and Nikes to update our shelves. It's Friday and I'm not due back at work until Monday morning, so I made up my mind to make sure my weekend wasn't ruined due to the mall robbery.

I turned on my TV and PlayStation, then hopped on 2K. I immediately saw that Ta'Juan was online playing as well. We hopped on an online PlayStation chat with our microphones connected to our controllers, so we could talk to each other as we played. The first thing Ta'Juan said was, "Aye nigga, did you see what happened at the mall," laughing as he spoke. "Yeah, that shit is crazy bro. I just left there less than an hour ago," I responded. We were playing a 2 vs 2 basketball pickup game online against some random players. The first team to reach twenty-one points wins. My virtual created player was about six foot five and played the point guard position. I called the plays, shot three-pointers, and had a decent mid-range jump shot as well. Ta'Juan's virtual player was a power forward. He was six foot ten and was mainly used for dunking, defense, and grabbing rebounds. He also had a decent mid-range jumper. Rolan called me on my cell phone as Ta'Juan and I were still playing NBA 2K so I didn't answer. I didn't want to be distracted from the game. A few minutes passed and then Rolan ended up joining our PlayStation party chat. I guess Ta'Juan sent him an invite. Rolan was quiet at first but then became more vocal during Ta'Juan and I's second game. Going on one of his random rants. "Stop referring yourself and other Black people niggas," he said. Ta'Juan and I both laughed. We always call Rolan an "old head" because he always talks like an old ass man. Sounding like somebody's uncle or grandpa. Rolan kept going in on us. "If a white man was to call you a nigga, you'd be mad, but when a Black man calls you a nigga, it's okay. Why is that?" Rolan asked us both. "Man, fuck all that. We niggas and the word nigga don't mean what it used to mean. Let a white man call me a nigga and I'll knock his fucking head off his shoulders," Ta'Juan said laughingly. I kind of agreed with Ta'Juan, which is rare. I finally spoke up, "This is crazy to say, but I agree with Ta'Juan on this one. Nigga is used today as a term of endearment. Niggas can say nigga, but white folks can't say it. That's just how it is." I hit the game-winning three-point shot while Rolan began to school us again with another unwanted lecture. "You can't hate the roots of a tree and not hate the tree. The demeaning, degrading, defiling word 'nigga' was a forced slur onto our people. The definition of a nigga is an ignorant person or someone who has no knowledge of self. Niggas are the weak-minded, hopeless, and defenseless people in this world. We're the aboriginal people to inhabit this earth. We're the first to step foot onto this planet. We come from divine ancestry. Why do y'all think they call Africa the motherland? They call it that because everything originates from Africa or from an African/Black individual. America, Russia, China, and the other so-called big powers of the world, would not be able to sustain their rule without exploiting Africa's resources, wealth, and people. Again, we are brothers and sisters. Kings and Queens. Goddesses and Gods. Not niggas, bitches, or hoes." I responded, "Yeah, you right bro," just to get him to shut up. I think Ta'Juan may have muted Rolan on his mic because he sent me a text that said, "let me know when Rolan done talking." Ta'Juan and I dominated every game we played online. "Nigga, we up by ten already! We gotta' run at least five more games before we call it a night," he said with excitement through his mic. I finally got off the game around 11 P.M. I smoked a blunt I had rolled up earlier that morning. I bought a zip from Ta'Juan a few days ago, so I wouldn't have to keep buying grams. I went to my refrigerator to warm up some leftover pasta from last night. I went out with this girl I met at the gas station. The pasta didn't taste so good, and the restaurant service was trash, but Tanya gave the best service a man could ask for later that night. I started to think about what Rolan was talking about as I lay on my bed smoking. I wasn't just thinking about what Rolan said, but also about all the shit Rolan lectures us about in general. Like how he said our last names don't belong to us. Instead, they belong to our forefathers' slave masters. "When we were forcefully brought to North America, the slave master stripped us of our original names and gave us their last names to denote that we were their property. A Black police officer sits at the top of the coon list. A coon or uncle tom is somebody that is Black and seeks to please white people. They crave white folks' attention, approval, and validation. They don't side with nor aim to help Black people in any way. They want to stay under the control of white America and their white power-structured government. When a Black police officer says he or she joined the police department to better serve, help, and protect my community and to catch bad guys, that's bullshit. Even if they have the best intentions to do so. I'll tell you why." Rolan continued, "The police formed in the 1800s to protect/control property and maintain law and order in America's society at a time when Blacks were considered property not people by law. There had to be ways to control Black people since chattel slavery ended. So, who are the police and law enforcement here to protect? Why is it that

Black people vote faithfully at every local, state, and presidential election but still receive nothing from the candidates or people in office? What real power do Black people have if we receive nothing tangible from the Black representation?"

Rolan has always had a love for books. Really for anything that touches on Black/African history, progression, and advancement. Just last week he linked with Brother Jamaal and told me all about what they talked about. He was telling Ta'Juan and me about how powerful melanin is. Melanin is our black or brown hair, the iris of the eye, skin pigmentation, or skin color. It is also intelligence that produces our unique abilities and talents as Black people. He always has a book in his hands. In the past, racist white folks made it illegal for Black people/Africans to know or try to learn how to read and write. It was punishable by death in the United States. We would have found out how powerful we are and how great unity was all we needed. We still need it today. He talked about how important women are to Black civilization. A group of people can rise no higher than its woman. I clicked one of the links Rolan texted me earlier of a Khallid Muhammad speech from the 90s. After watching that one I began to see suggested videos of other Black figures. Minister Nuri Muhammad was a well-known and wise minister who preached almost everything Rolan spoke about. Spreading the black dollar by creating, owning, and operating businesses and services instead of relying on people who oppressed us, and still do today, to sustain our everyday needs. Why would you expect the same system and power which have led you to your current issues and problems to help you? Rolan also sent me links to Dr. Umar Johnson. Dr. Umar Johnson is just as funny as intelligent. He also put me on Brother Ben X, Dick Gregory, Huey P. Newton, Assata Shakur, Brother Rizza Islam, Dick Gregory, Angela Davis, Khallid Muhammad, Sista Souljah, John Henrik Clarke, Dr. Claud Anderson, Michelle Alexander, Minister Louis Farrakhan, and a few others. Also, many Malcolm X speeches and lectures. He even gave me The Autobiography of Malcolm X. I haven't read it yet though. I thought it would be some boring shit, but it was interesting to see how confident and powerful these Black men and women are and how unapologetic they are about being Black. Within their history and culture. It was around 1 A.M. once I got done watching all the links. I didn't even notice how fast time was flying by. I had learned so much. I began to instantly feel good. This sudden urge to conduct some type of action came upon me. I just didn't know what to do exactly.

I decided to finally hop in the shower. I made sure to bring my speaker. I always listen to music in the shower. I had Brent Fiyaz's "Wasteland" album on full blast. I got out of the shower, dried off, headed back to my bed, and put my phone on the charger. I was tired and high. I immediately passed out in bed.

Chapter Three

Damn

I woke up the next morning later than usual. I naturally woke up around 7 A.M. but was up at 9 A.M. this day. That wasn't the only unusual thing that happened. I got a random phone call from somebody that wasn't in my contacts. The phone buzzed as I was half asleep and half too dazed to figure out where my phone was. It had fallen between my bed and the wall, so I was digging my hand between the head of my bed and the wall feeling my hand blindly for my phone. I finally found it. I picked it up and I answered with a drowsy "Hello?" A smooth voice answered with a sharp quickness. "Good morning, this is Officer James McKinn. I'm with the Indianapolis Metro Police Department. Am I speaking with Joel Jackson?" He sounded all nice and happy to be speaking with me, but we all know that's one of the trick tactics cops use. I hesitated to answer him. You would think a police officer would call from an unknown number, but it was a normal 317 Indianapolis area code. I had no idea why a police officer was calling me, but I didn't care. I hung up the phone as quickly as it had rung. He called back immediately. I let it ring until he hung up. Then I blocked his number.

I got dressed then walked to the living room and sat on my couch. I threw on a red sweat suit I got from H&M and these grey Pumas with a white Puma decal. I went through my

Instagram and Twitter to get updates on what's new in the world. It's kind of like the new way of reading the morning paper to catch up on everything going on. Gas prices are still high, GloRilla sold 200,000 copies of her newest albums already and the Pacers won their game last night. On the local level, a girl I used to kick it with passed away last night. I can't remember her name cause it's been forever since we last talked, but I'll always remember her face because she had a birthmark shaped like a oval on her right cheek. There were a lot of "RIP," "Rest Easy" and "Gone way too soon" tweets and post with a picture of her down my timeline.

I checked my Instagram direct message or DM and saw my nigga Travis had messaged me. He told me to text him ASAP, so I did. He told me about how he wasn't doing too well in college so now he is looking for a job just in case he has to drop out of college. He was attending Indiana State University. Travis was an All-American athlete in high school. He was an All-American football, basketball, and track star. He had partial scholarships to a hand full of Division 1 colleges across the country. He went to Indiana State to be closer to his sick mother. He's currently a sophomore. I told him I'll ask Rey when I get back to work. I have always been against college. I had a 1.5 GPA in high school, so I never even considered being a college student. Degrees don't even hold any weight. Used to be able to get a degree and find a good job instantly but not anymore. Mainly stemming from Black folks in recent years obtaining degrees more than ever. Once we started getting degrees, the value in them went down to corporate America. You sit through overpriced lectures and classes just for you to obtain a piece of paper or "degree" with your name on it. The goal is to go to college to get a good job when you graduate but that is not the case for many Black college graduates. College is supposed to provide valuable education and information that can improve your overall quality of life. Black graduates end up in so much debt that even if they find a decent job, they are living the next twenty years paying off that debt. I don't know what I want to be or do in life, but I know I'm not ending up in debt for a piece of paper. Shit, I'll slap your name on a piece of paper for $20 and a high five. If I pay $900 for a new phone and I can't make a phone call or sent a text message then that would be considered a faulty product. I should be able to get a refund. I believe the same thing when it comes to college. If you want to be a doctor, lawyer, or something like that I understand but anything else, fuck college.

I cut my living room TV on and turned to ESPN. My phone rang. Somebody was facetiming me. It was Bernice. Me and her chill now and then. We last fucked the weekend before last. We never go out we just chill at my crib. I knew she was more than likely wanting to see what I was doing that night. I answered. "Wassup." She giggled the answered, "Hey love, what are you doing tonight?" she asked in a seductive voice. She had the camera angled on her face and breasts. I gave a smooth response. "Shit, I'm coming to yo' crib tonight." She laughed. "Ummhmm, who said you can come over here?" she blushed. She then continued, "I'm just playing you know you always welcome at my spot. Be here by nine o'clock." I responded, "Bet," and then hung up the phone. I headed to the kitchen to make some cereal. I always keep a box of my favorite, cinnamon toast crunch.

I grabbed a plastic bowl and a plastic spoon from my small pantry. I hate washing dishes, so I always use plastic bowls, plates, and other utensils. As soon as I was about to grab the box of cereal sitting above my fridge my phone rang again! This time it was Ta'Juan. "You tryna go to this party tonight?" he asked. "Who all gone be there?" I asked. "I don't know, it's just some shit one of my hoes told me about," he said. I didn't want to slide to another party after what happened during the last one we went to. It got shot up because some nigga was upset about a girl he wanted talked to one of his ops. "Nah, I'm good bro. I ain't tryna' fuck with a party tonight," I said. "Damn, Rolan said the same shit. His ass said he tryna' finish a new book he got. But ight I'll catch you later," Ta'Juan said. "Cool be safe bro," I responded then hung up the phone.,

I finished my cereal, brushed my teeth, brushed my hair, and changed into my Jordan Bred 11s. I stepped out, locked up my apartment, then hopped in my car and headed to the mall. Some new Jordans came out; all-black retro Jordan 3's. I forgot about the robbery at the mall until I was reminded once I pulled up. I parked at the front entrance of the mall where customers normally do since I wasn't working that day. As I walked up to the front entrance, I noticed small pieces of glass on the ground near the front main entrance of the mall. It wasn't a lot but it was enough to where you could tell somebody did a half-assed job cleaning it up. The two doors at the main entrance were in perfect condition. Soon as I walked in, social media confirmed everything. I saw five stores boarded up due to being broken into. Three stores remained open. Target, Victoria's Secret, and Vick's. I walked into Vick's and said wassup' to Rey. He dapped me up. "Them J's comes in yet?" I asked.

"Nah they said the truck not coming today because of the robbery. I and a new guy I hired last week cleaned up the store. That's why no customers are here now. We had a few customers earlier who just looked around but didn't buy anything. Ah yeah, Sarah is here too but she on break," he said. Sarah is this cool white girl that been working at Vick's for about two months now. She's tall with blonde hair and probably has just as many shoes as I do. "And some girl came in asking for you. She described you to a T so I knew she was asking about you. I don't who she was tho," Rey said. I didn't either so I thought nothing of it. I looked around for a little bit to see if some all-white Air Force Ones had come in. Wanted to get some for my Pops. The funny thing is he is only 5 foot 5 but wears a size eleven in shoes. I copped him a pair, dapped up Rey, then cut out. I was walking out of Vick's when I heard a familiar voice calling out for me. "Joel!" she yelled. I looked over my right shoulder and there she was. I put two and two together and realized that it had to be the girl that found my wallet but only this time she wasn't wearing her purple coat covering her face. She was speed-walking up to me. Her high-pitched voice made hers distinguishable from anyone else's. I could now see all of her as the mall lights shined on her graceful beauty. She was cheesin' from ear to ear as she approached me. I was wondering how she knew my name. We were standing in front of Vick's. Her back was to the store, and I stood in front of her. I could see Rey smiling as he walked from the back to the front of the store to ear hustle and listen to our conversation. He tried to pretend he was folding clothes near the store entrance, but I knew what he was doing. She continued, "You lucky I'm a nice girl. I could have easily stolen your ID and debit card if I wanted to. I still can't believe you didn't realize you dropped it," she said as she laughed. She grinned then said, "My name is Deja by the way." I remember being amazed by her smile. Her pearly white teeth complimented her rich dark skin. She was a true elegant beauty. Her hair was flawless. She had locs that went down to her shoulders. She was a few inches shorter than me. Around 5'1 or 5'2, which makes me feel taller than I am. I finally responded, "I appreciate you, Deja. That's crazy, I had no idea I had dropped it." "Yeah, you owe me now," she said still smiling. I responded, "Let me show my appreciation. What you got going on tonight? I'd like to take you out." I told her looking directly into her eyes. She blushed. It was kind of funny because she tried to hide it by looking down and faking a cough. I have always been straight up and forward with women. No reason to beat around the bush. "Umm, I don't know yet. I was planning to go see a movie by myself since I don't have any friends," she said. I took that as a hint that she's not doing anything tonight. I had to play my cards exactly right. I didn't want to sound too desperate, but then I still had to show her that I was interested in her. I responded with "I was gone slide to a party with the guys tonight, but honestly, I'd rather spend my time getting to know you better. Let's go see a movie together. You can pick the movie when we get there." That was a lie. I wasn't planning to go to that party, but I had to make it seem like I was changing my plans for her. She smiled widely and agreed to meet up with me. "Yeah, I guess that's okay," she said blushing again. This time she didn't try to hide it. I pulled my phone out. "Let me get your number. Or at least your Instagram." I handed her my phone. She grabbed it and said, "Here you go," as she sent herself a text message from my phone to hers of her Instagram name. Now I had her number and Instagram name. I followed her on Instagram, but I didn't get a good look at her full profile page at that exact moment. "I'll be free around 6 P.M.," she said. "Bet, I'll pick you up then," I responded. She said that she didn't need a ride and would meet me at the movie theater located right behind the mall.

I was headed out of the mall to the parking lot. Before I could walk out the main entrance, an older white man stopped me. He wore khakis, a red collared shirt tucked into his pants, a trench coat, cropped military-style buzz cut, a clean-shaven face, and dark shades. "Good morning Mr. Joel, I'm Officer Mckinns. We spoke briefly over the phone earlier this morning. Do you have time to talk?" As he spoke, he put his hands on his hips moving his jacket back a little. His badge could be seen clinging to his hip right by his service pistol. I still have no idea how he got my name and phone number. I thought about ignoring him and just keep walking but when I ignored his questions over the phone earlier, he just pulled up on me out of the blue so I might as well get it over with. I answered his questions about where I was last night, what time did I leave Vick's, did I see any suspicious activity in the mall, and where I went after I left the mall. He took my words down into his small notepad and thanked me for answering his line of questions. He walked further into the mall towards the store that had been hit and I walked out.

I finally left the mall. I was driving on the highway when Pops texted me asking if I had been saving my money. I never save money. I'm always going out to eat, mainly at fast food spots, buying shoes, buying clothes, and spending my last few dollars on weed so that only leaves me with a few dollars left over. Inflation is not helping either. Gas is high, food is high, and rent is high. Used to be able to go to the grocery store instead of eating out to save money but now it makes no difference. The cost of daily life essentials is rising but wages aren't. I told him I was trying to save, but shit keeps coming up. Rent going up, high gas prices, had to get new brakes the other day, and other shit. Pops reminded me that he made some mistakes back in the day, so he's doing his best to make sure I don't make those same mistakes. Financial mistakes, criminal mistakes, and more. "Love you son" was the last thing he texted me after his lecture. "Love you too Pops," I responded. I cut on Young Dolphs mixtape "16 Zips" mixtape to play for the last few minutes I had left until I was due to arrive home. I only live 10 minutes away from the mall. I was about two songs into the mixtape and five minutes away from the crib when my phone rang again. It was Bernice. I pulled up to a red traffic light. "Fuck" is all I could say to myself. I forgot I had originally planned to hang out with her. I answered her call. "Hey, love! I forgot, are you coming to my apartment or am I coming to yours?" she asked before I could even get a word out. I responded, "Wassup. My fault, but something came up tonight. I won't be able to come through." She sucked her teeth in irritation then hung up the phone just like that. I was pulling into the entrance of my apartment complex when she sent me multiple angry text messages saying how I'm not shit and how I'm just like these other broke ass niggas she fucks with. I left her on read.

It was close to 4 pm when I began cleaning up my apartment. Deja had also texted me at 4:15 P.M. about the movie she wants to go see. It was called *A wasteful love.* I swept and mopped the floor, vacuumed, cleaned the bathroom, organized, and put away everything that was randomly lying around. I also took out the trash.

I finally checked out her Instagram profile on my phone, since she texted me her profile earlier at the mall. From one of her recent posts, I found out she is a year older than me. I looked more through her page and found out she attends Nivy Tech, a local community college, to become a psychologist. She also loves to sing from a few videos of her singing on her page. I also clicked the YouTube link in her bio. She had one original song but most of her video uploads are covers of popular songs like Summer Walker *Girls Need Love*, Arri Lenox *She Butter Baby*, SZA *Far*, and Anita Baker *Sweet Love*.

It was 5 P.M. so I headed to the gas station to clean out my car and get some gas. I texted Deja, "Omw," meaning that I was on my way. She texted back, "Okay see you soon," with a smiley face emoji. I pulled up to the movie theater and parked my car in the nearly packed parking lot, then walked into the main entrance of the theater. It was jam-packed. I was nervous that tickets would be sold out. I don't know why I didn't think to buy them ahead of time online so we are guaranteed seats. I approached the counter to purchase tickets. "Good evening, what movie will you be seeing tonight?" the lady inside a glass ticket booth asked. I responded, "Two tickets for the 6 P.M. showing of A Wasteful Love please, thank you." I pulled out my wallet for my debit card, tapped it on the machine, and she slid me two tickets through a small opening on the front glass casing of the ticket booth. I stood inside by the front entry door in the heat looking outside for Deja. I waited for ten minutes before I saw her walking up from the parking lot. I didn't see her pull up. She was a few minutes late, but I wasn't trippin'. The movie had already started ten minutes ago but it was cool because previews of upcoming movies always play before the actual movie starts. I held the door open as she was slowly getting closer to the entrance. "Hey, I'm so sorry my Uber was late picking me up. I'm having some car troubles," she said in a cute and sincere way. "It's all good. I'm just glad to see you again. I already have our tickets so let's head in," I said. She immediately gave a big smile but showed no teeth in an attempt to hold back her blush. I had already purchased tickets, so I showed the man at the front stand, a few feet to the entry point, both tickets. He looked at them to confirm then said, "You two are in room 12 and your seats are G11 and G12." I gave one to Deja. The concessions were by the arcade filled with all types of snacks and drinks. I could see Deja looking at the concessions. "You want a snack or something for the movie?" I asked to be nice but honestly was hoping she said no. They be charging $20 for some popcorn, and I only had about $150 in my bank account. She kept looking at the concessions as she responded, "I'm good I just get lost in space sometimes," she said with a giggle. I smiled. She continued, "Oh, I almost forgot to tell you that I picked up a few snacks from the gas station on my way here. Watermelon sour patches, Hot Cheetos, and two water bottles. It's all in my purse. I hope you like those. My phone died so I could ask what you wanted," she said. "That's coo'. I'll just eat a few of each. I appreciate you cause' they really be taxing here for snacks," I said. There was a small game room to the right of the lobby. It had normal games like Pac-Man, Galaga, Street Fighter, and more.

We finally walked into our movie showing room. I held the door open for her, which brought a blushing smile to her lovely face. We walked in and headed up the steps to take our seats. As we were walking the lights began to dim indicating the movie was soon to start. Section A at the lower section of the theater close to the screen up to the K section at the top. We were in section G. I was ahead of her until we got to our section and I let her sit down first. We took our seats. She immediately reclined hers back. As did I. She was very excited to do so like a little girl getting a new doll to play with. We made it just in time. The previews were over, so the movie was just now beginning. She leaned her head over to me and whispered, "I've been waiting for this movie to drop for years now! The book was really good, so I hope the movie is too." Now that I think about it, I do remember seeing her post a lot about books she's read on Instagram. The movie we were seeing was one of those romantic chick flicks. I saw the trailer once on Twitter. I pretended to be interested in the movie at first just to be nice. I'm not a fan of these types of movies. But as began watching, I realized it was kind of good. I even thought of maybe buying the book.

I accidentally fell asleep mid-way through the movie. I woke up and the movie was over with the credits still rolling. Deja put the armrest between us up and was leaning over on my chest. She was staring at the screen tearing up. She was so caught up in the movie that I don't even think she noticed I fell asleep. She wiped her falling tears, sniffed her nose, gained her composure, and said, "The book was amazing, but the movie was even better." I responded, "I'm surprised to hear that because normally I hear people say the book is better than the movie." She got up from my chest and un-reclined her seat. The theater lights came back on as the credits were rolling. "You good?" I asked. She smiled and then shook her head signaling she was okay. We both got up to leave the room. I checked my phone as we walked down the steps toward the exit. I had a missed call from Rolan and an Instagram DM from Ta'Juan. I decided I'd call Rolan back later. I opened the DM from Ta'Juan. He sent a video of the party he was at. It was lit! Fine women everywhere! I closed my phone and we got up from our seats. We went down the steep steps and walked out of the showing room into the lobby area. Deja had looked over at me, then at my phone as I viewed the video again from Ta'Juan. "Hey how do you know Ta'Juan?" she asked me with slight excitement. "He's a good friend of mine," I said. I began to wonder how she knew Ta'Juan. Deja responded, "Oh really? We went to high school together. He's always been a funny guy. He used to make everybody laugh," she said. I thought to myself, I have never noticed her from high school. Did she recognize me? I just came out and straight up asked her as we were walking out of the room and into the theater lobby.

"So, you went to the same high school as us? I never seen you before." She responded, "Yeah, I remember seeing you in the halls with Ta'Juan and Rolan. I never said anything because I was too shy. I still am. Sorry if I'm being weird." Her eyes were innocent and sweet. She was blushing like she always does, but this time it was stronger than usual. If I would have known a sweet and genuine girl like Deja had a crush on me back in high school, I would have approached her. The crushes I had back in high school are all down bad. They're either out of shape, got a whole bunch of kids, or just don't do anything in real life besides looking good for social media. I think it's sad how so many people try to hold onto high school popularity after they graduate.

We were standing in the movie theater lobby by the arcade when I began asking her questions to get to know her better. "So, what are you studying in school?" Even though I saw it already saw it on her Instagram. Just needed to do something to get a conversation started. She responded "Well, I've always wanted to be a psychologist and a social worker. I was adopted when I was six, so I want to involve myself in a field to assist unwanted youth or youth that just need a shoulder to lean on. Also, I love being around kids! I plan to have a few someday in the future." Music began to play in the lobby. Deja sang along as the song blasted through the lobby speakers. I had never heard the song before. Her voice was like an angel. "What song is this?" I asked. She giggled. "It's called *love on the brain* by Rihanna," she said. This was the first time I had ever shown the slightest of real genuine interest in a girl. Aside from being purely sexual. It was something about her that made her different from the others. I just didn't quite know what it was, but I loved whatever it was. In the brief time that we have known each other, I already wanted to see her again after tonight.

I offered to give her a ride home since she came to the theater in an Uber. "No, it's okay. I'll just wait for another Uber but thank you for asking," she said as she pulled out her phone. "Dang, I forgot my phone died," you could hear how upset she was from the tone of her voice. She stood there thinking for a few seconds then said, "I'm so sorry. If it's not too late, can I take you up on that ride home please?" I responded, "Of course." She smiled. "Thanks. I really appreciate it," she said. I kindly asked her to wait inside the lobby by the entry door. It was cold so I didn't want her to have to walk too far in the freezing temperatures. "I'll be back in two seconds. I drive a grey 2001 impala," I said to her as she nodded in confirmation. I pushed through the entry doors and sped to my car. I pulled my car up and she jumped in after sprinting from the entry door. I laughed. “Dang, I didn’t even get a chance to hold the door open for you,” I told her jokingly. She was shivering as she got in. She laughed as well. “Sorry, I’m anemic. Thank you again for the ride home,” she said. “You hungry?” I asked. “I could eat,” she said. I knew the perfect place to take her.

I turned the heat up as high as it could go. She’s lucky I just got the heat in my car fixed a few days ago. I had the song *Sure Thing* by Miguel playing when she got in. She didn’t mind that only the right side of my car speakers worked. She was still vibing to the music. The song eventually came to an end. She talked about how much she loved R&B. She shyly asked if she could pick a song as we approached a red light. Without any words, I smirked and handed her my phone. During the fifteen-minute car ride, she played almost every song I had on my R&B playlist. We listened to about ten seconds of each song just to test each other’s musical taste. “What you know about this?” We would constantly say that to each other as we shot each other looks with laughter. It was only a ten-minute ride, but I enjoyed every second. Felt like an hour-long ride.

We finally pulled up to the soul food place. It’s called *Aboriginal Eats.* We walked into the restaurant and were seated by our waitress. It was slow that night, so we were greeted and seated by our waitress in no time. I checked my phone as Deja and I were looking over the menus. “I’m going to the bathroom real quick. I’ll be back,” I said to her. As I was on my way to the bathroom, my phone started to ring. “Hello?” I spoke. “Peace brother, how you doing?” Rolan said in a calm voice. “Shit I’m good nigga. I’m just out with this girl I met at the mall. Her name is Deja,” I said. “Deja Noles? She dark skin with locs?” Rolan asked. “Yeah,” I answered Rolan, “how you know her?” Rolan answered “I remember here from High School. She used to sing the national anthem for all the football and basketball games.” I can’t believe I never realized that was her. “Damn, now that I think about it, that was her,” I said. “Yeah, she hard, but I called just to check up on you brotha. Just wondering if you had a chance to watch that speech I sent you a few days ago. But I ain’t mean to interrupt your date,” Rolan said. “You good bro, I’m in the bathroom right now but Imma’ talk to you later about that. I actually watched it plus more videos.” I responded. “That’s great to hear brother! Also, I’m nobody’s nigga. Neither are you. You shouldn't even be referring to yourself as a nigga. But we'll talk later bro," he said, then hung up the phone.

I used the bathroom, washed my hands, and headed back to Deja. The waitress was standing by the table talking to Deja. Looked like they were having the time of their life laughing and giggling. "My fault, I didn't expect the phone call to be that long," I said to both Deja and the waitress. "Oh, it's okay Joel, no need to be sorry," Deja said with a smile on her face. Deja and the waitress shot each other a look as they smiled. I'm sure they were talking about me when I was away from the table. From the feel of the vibe, I could tell it had to be about something good. She finally took our order. Deja ordered lemon pepper chicken wings with corn bread and a side of macaroni. I ordered the same thing but with a side of coleslaw. Deja giggled. I guess my asking for coleslaw was funny to her. I could tell Deja was enjoying herself, which made me feel good. I must admit, I had never had this much fun with a girl before. I know we just went to the movies and are grabbing something to eat, but there is something about Deja that makes me want to keep seeing her again in the future. I don't just enjoy looking at her, but I enjoy being in her presence and witnessing her unique grace.

I was done eating well before Deja was finished. I always thought it was funny how some girls try to look fake pretty when they eat but Deja was not one of them. She was eating like she was at the crib. I liked that about her. The waitress handed me the bill. Once Deja was finished eating, I paid and tipped the waitress. I checked my phone paying for our date. I had $895 in my bank account. I forgot Rey paid us early this week plus a $100 bonus due to staff appreciation week.

I held the door open for Deja as we headed out of the restaurant. We walked to my car. I opened the passenger door for her. She smiled and then leaned over to me to give me a gentle kiss on the cheek. I was smiling hard. Felt a little weird because I'm normally smooth when it comes to women, but I felt like I was off my game tonight. But as long as Deja wasn't complaining about anything I knew I was all right. I closed her door then walked around the car and hopped in the driver's seat. She asked for my phone to type in her parents' house. "I know everybody wants to move out, but I stay with my parents to save money until I graduate from college," she said. It was only about five minutes away from where I stayed. I wasn't even pressed about trying to get her to come to the crib like some weirdos do. Sex is not everything. I've gone out with hundreds of girls, but Deja was different. She grabbed the aux and played music. She played GloRilla, Beyonce, and Megan Thee Stallion. I took the long way to her house which added an extra eight minutes so we could listen to more songs. I know Deja noticed but didn't mind at all. We enjoyed each other's company. As I was pulling up in front of her parent's driveway, I noticed how big their driveway was. The house wasn't all that big, but the driveway was crazy. As soon as I parked in front of her crib, she gave me a hug along with, "I really enjoyed spending time with you tonight." "Same here beautiful," I said. "Text me when you get home," she said as she got out of the car, shut the door, and made her way up the long narrow driveaway. I stayed watching to make sure she got in safely. I pulled off once her front door opened. I had no more than a seven-minute drive back home due to the absence of traffic.

Chapter Four

Supreme Wisdom

Rolan was invited to speak at a community outreach event aiming to stop the violence and murder rate throughout Indianapolis. Last year, we had a record number of murders in our city; 281 were killed. With the way this year is coming to an end, we may surpass that number. The program was called "Act now or suffer later!" The flyer had been shared on social media for last past few weeks. The event was to be held at our old high school gymnasium. Rolan has a decent following on Instagram and subscribers on YouTube as a result of his Black empowerment, advancement, re-educational, and overall Black progression content. He has some clout or popularity throughout the city for his podcast called "Black progression." He just talks about how we as Black people need our own political party, land, accesses to wealth, economic structure, businesses, providing services, and more. The speakers for the event included a few community leaders, ministers, nationally known entrepreneurs, activists, and parents of some of a few murder victims.

Rolan called Ta'Juan and I on a group Facetime. Rolan emphasized making sure Ta'Juan and I were dressed in business casual style. The only pair of dress shoes I had were these brown shoes my grandma bought for my high school graduation. Ta'Juan was not happy about Rolan wanting us to dress up. He pleaded his case that a Burberry collared shirt, jeans, Timbs, or some crisp Jordans were business casual enough. "My nigga, are we going to hear you speak, or are we going to an Easter Sunday church service? Why the fuck I can't wear some fly shit like I normally do?" Ta'Juan said as I laughed at his response. I couldn't help it. Rolan however, did not find any humor in Ta'Juan's opposition. Rolan responded, "I want the individuals in attendance to see us dressed like we mean business. We don't want to be taken as a joke. Look and carry ourselves in a way that will be a positive reflection of ourselves, our people, and our goal. I say "our" instead of just my goal because I hope you two join me one day in the effort to liberate our people."

Since the first time I met Rolan, he has been hounding Ta'Juan and me about a term called knowledge of self. When I initially heard the term knowledge of self, I thought it was referring to knowing what I want to do or be in life. Similar to how high school counselors try to force you to pick a career path at 17 or 18 years old. Rolan enlightened me about what it meant. Knowledge of self is gaining a thorough understanding of the infinite history and identity of our people. Knowing your history helps you solve your current issues or problems, which then ensures a better future. Almost any problem today has happened in the past in some way, shape, or form. Our history doesn't begin in chains or with slavery. The American school system will never teach you about that. Black/African history goes farther back than any other racial group of people in human existence. When you gain knowledge, valuable education, and information, that then produces inspiration. This is best achieved when learning about your people, their achievements, and their unique abilities. We wouldn't need an anti-lynching bill or law if the mental lynching didn't happen in the classrooms. If you learn about great things our people did, people that look like you, then you will think of yourself in a positive light. You can relate and share something in common. If you learn about the great things people who don't look like you did plus negative things about people who look like you, then you will look at yourself in a negative light. If you realize it or not. You then use the newly acquired information and inspiration to better your overall quality of life. Which then you can help your people. It is also referred to as racial pride. Racial pride links to happiness, success, and power. Real tangible, economic, and political power. Power to control our own decisions and destiny as Black people. Not having to vote or depend on a government that has a five-hundred-year history of not doing right by Black people to do anything in our best interest. You can use whatever you do or involve yourself in as a tool towards achieving true Black liberation. Also known as freedom. Colin Kaepernick used his NFL platform to spread awareness of police brutality against Black people. Malcolm X used his speaking skills and profound intellect to give Black people a Black economic philosophy. Dick Gregory used his comedy skills and intellect to instill courage and determination into Black people. Kyrie Irving and Lebron James use their platforms gained from being in the NBA to educate, motivate and empower Black people. LeBron James even created the I Promise School and other endeavors. Angela Davis used her scholarly skills to educate our people. Maya Angelou used her writing skills to inspire and entertain our people. Knowing your history and having a sense of racial pride motivates and inspires you to not just want more, but to get more in life. History also can hinder you from falling for the same tricks, false promises, and lies Black people/African have fallen victim to for centuries at the hands of our oppressors. Racist Europeans and white Americans throughout the years and still today, have given us a falsified identity of what a Black man and woman is and should be. They deliberately indoctrinate or brainwash Black people to feel, think, and act with inferiority. They purposely twist or lie about our history to hinder us from aspiring to do better in life. Recently, Kyrie Irving was under fire for posting a link from Amazon to a film that has been deemed offensive to Jewish people today. He was suspended from the NBA, lost his Nike endorsement, millions of dollars, and grilled by white controlled media outlets. Why was Amazon not attacked when they refused to remove it from their website? Why is Nike taking the so called moral high road when they have child laborers? NFL Hall of Famer Brett Favre stole millions from welfare and poor people across America to fund his daughter's volleyball facility but faced no legal action or repercussions. UFC President Dana White slapped his wife on camera in front of a dozen witnesses but has faced no consequences. I wonder why not?

If the American government is successful at erasing the evil acts committed against Black people in the past, then we won't be able to detect the present issues. They inflict sufferings not just on Black people in America but the masses of Black people across the globe. The first thing they did was separate Africans or Black people from their families, their culture, and their heritage, and kill their African identity. They replaced it with white/European values and beliefs. Imagine a family with a mother, a father, and a son. The son has been forcefully taken away from his family. The boy is more likely to not know anything about his family now that he has been stripped from his roots, his heritage. It is more than likely that he will be unable to tell you where he comes from, his ancestry, his culture, religion, language, spiritual beliefs, etc. This gives the oppressors the opportunity to instill whatever inferior beliefs or views onto the young impressionable child since he has never been taught the truth about himself. He has no self-esteem or aspiration to learn about his people or history since he is being lied to by the oppressor and their institutions. If you have no knowledge of the great things your people have done, you will think they have done nothing important which begins to make you believe you can't do anything great. The boy will believe anything his oppressors tell him since there is nothing or no one to debate what he is being taught. James Baldwin once said, "A child cannot be taught by anyone who despises him." Assata Shakur once said, "Slaves were encouraged to take the misery of their lives out on each other instead of the master. The slave masters taught us we were ugly, less than human, unintelligent, and many of us believed it." You can't expect a government or group of people who lied, killed, enslaved, raped, and exploited your people to have the best intentions when it comes to your overall well-being.

The media has always been against African/ Black people. Remember that Black people or African Americans are members of the African people. We share the same history and African genotype. Characteristics like hair texture, skin complexion, nose, and abilities. America's history books and media have done their best to try to separate Africans from being Black people and Black people from being Africans. When I was younger, I remember seeing commercials about Africa being a third-world country, having no food or water for its people. They were told to be running around naked with spears and knives. In the history books in most middle schools and high schools, they begin talking about Africans starting off as slaves. Africans are the aboriginal people to inhabit this earth. We are glorious and divine beings.

Some people don't believe Black people can come together in mass to achieve something great. Well, we have not too long ago. The Reconstruction Era took place in the late 1800s and early 1900s in America. It was the most progressive period in Black history; Black-owned everything, and we were doing everything for ourselves. We were self-reliant people. There were Black-owned banks, Black health clinics, schools, transportation companies, grocery stores, and more. White terror and The Civil Rights Movement to a certain extent initiated the downfall of Black-owned everything. It was a period of great cohesiveness but no real progression besides laws or words on paper that are no better than the people who abide by them. Hence the quote by the great Dr. Martin Luther King Jr during the final years of his life, "I fear I may have integrated my people into a burning house." Integration during the Civil Rights Movement caused Blacks/Africans to join white American businesses, which subsequently meant abandoning our businesses. It wasn't just a social integration such as being able to go to a sporting event, movie, or restaurant with white people, but it was, more importantly, an economic integration. It's not racist to say Black people need to separate from white people. I'm not saying we need to begin a social separation from white people. Having white friends and associates is your choice. There needs to be an economic, political, and psychological separation. Each racial group of people has different needs, concerns, and interests.

It was now time to get dressed for the community meeting. I threw on a simple white button-down, black slacks, and brown dress shoes from my high school graduation. I pulled up to Ta'Juan's house around 10 A.M. Ta'Juan is always fresh from head to toe but has no car. I keep telling him he needs to get his priorities together. Rolan wanted us to be there and seated by 10:30 A.M. The program started at 11 A.M. I texted him, "I'm outside," so he would come out. He argued with his baby momma as he walked out the front door and locked it. By Ta'Juan's appearance, it looked as if he had forgotten everything Rolan said in our conversation. He was wearing an Armani coat on top of a grey Armani collared shirt which had red and white trim around the color. He rocked some retro fire red Jordan 4's to top it all off with some light blue fitted jeans. He hopped in my car, smelling like a weed shop. I couldn't believe Ta'Juan thought it would be okay to enter a High School smelling like weed, but I still to this day remind myself that not everyone was raised the same as me. "Aye bro, you a grown ass man. I can't make you do anything, but you know we about to go to a High School full of kids and parents. Why would you think it's okay to walk into a High School smelling like weed? Plus, did you listen to anything Rolan told you his morning about what you should wear?" I said to him. He just shrugged his shoulders and disregarded everything I had just said. "Fuck it," I responded. Then pulled off to head to the event.

We finally got to our former High School for the community event. It was packed; every seat in the bleachers was filled. They had to pull out chairs from the school cafeteria and pass those out to seat everybody. The only reason Ta'Juan and I got seats was become Rolan reserved them for us. As soon as we walked in, an older lady at the door greeted us. She handed us a pamphlet with the guest speakers' information and a flyer for a local organization called The Panthers Revived. At first, I thought it was referring to the Marvel Black Panther superhero from Wakanda but when I googled The Panthers Revived their Instagram popped up. I clicked the website link in their profile bio. It gave a quick history of the original militant group called the Self Armed Defense Black Panther Party. The Panther Revived was inspired by the original Black Panther Party. Between the 1960s and 70s, there was a movement that took place which is referred to as the Black Power movement. Many know about the civil rights movement, but what about the Black Panther Party which took place doing the Black Power era? This movement and organization of Black men and women led by Huey P. Newton had the same aim and goal as the civil rights movement, to liberate and better the overall quality of life of the masses of Black people but had a different stance and approach. The Black Panthers were armed and militant. They followed the philosophy and ideals of Malcolm X closely. Fun fact, they were originally going to call themselves the Sons of Malcolm before settling on the name Black Panthers. Also, they believed Black people should always be armed or obtain firearms to protect their lives against police brutality, the KKK, and other white supremacist groups and institutions. They also believed in community involvement and re-education. They created health clinics, a free breakfast program, passed out literature and books to educate the people, and more. The idea for the WIC (Women, Infants, and Children) government assistance program came from the Black Panther's free breakfast program for Black and minority families.

There was a rectangular stage in the middle of the gymnasium. It consisted of two large pieces that meet together in the middle. It took a four-man team to put it together. I know because I used to help put it together before the high school pep rallies. A tall brown podium stood in the middle of the stage towards the front. The packed bleachers were fifty feet away from the stadium. The speakers for the event sat in chairs ten feet behind the podium in a line. Hundreds of extra chairs sat across from the stage for spectators who could not fit into the bleachers. Ta'Juan and I sat towards the front of the stage in the third row of chairs.

Our former vice principal, now the current principal, Mr. Donley, gave a few words to kick off the program. He was the only one who fought to keep Mr. Stenson a few years back. He stood at the podium in a red suit jacket, black dress pants, a white dress shirt, and a black tie. "It is with great honor and gratitude that I graciously thank our wonderful speakers for taking time out of their hectic schedules to be here and also to the members of the audience for coming out to support the struggle and efforts to change the condition of our people on this glorious Saturday morning," he said. As he ended his sentence, he began to clap along with the speakers and members of the audience joining in. Once the applause ended, he got back into it by naming each speaker. There was a slight pause between each name as the crowd applauded with approval: "Michelle Alexander (applause) Nuri Muhammad (applause) Dr. Umar Johnson (applause) Brother Rizza Islam (applause) Rolan Shabazz." Mr. Donley then invited the first speaker to the podium. "The powerful, eloquent, and mighty revolutionary himself, Dr. Umar Johnson. Please join me in a round of applause as he makes his way to the podium," the crowd clapped along with him. Dr. Umar Johnson is a well-known psychologist, activist, and Pan-African. He has a strong social media presence and following, which has propelled his status as a great activist. He is also creating his own school geared towards African/Black-focused curriculums. Dr. Umar almost immediately grabbed the audience with his heavy words. He talked about the negative social and psychological effects inflicted on our people due to white brainwashing. I can't remember everything he said word for word, but I do remember most of what he said. Basic standardized tests that school systems mandate their students to take are proven to be against Black students. Another tactic in support of widening the gap between white and Black students. We need internal reparations before external reparations. He also said reparations are well deserved for the masses of Black people, but we don't need them. Black people are a trillion-dollar economy each year.

Let's be honest, some of our people wouldn't know how to properly handle reparations. If we got reparations tomorrow, some would spend it on white-owned designer brands. Gucci purses and slides, Armani jeans, Loui Vuitton belts, Versace sunglasses, etc. Buying cars at high interest rates, strip clubs, 24-inch rims on a car with its engine light on, and more. We lead all racial groups of people when it comes to unnecessary spending, so there would need to be some re-education on how to become producers and invest in ourselves. Spend our hard-earned Black dollars on our own. We have to learn financial behaviors that will lead to Black ownership and enterprise. But then again, you have to remember that everybody can't come to the promised land. All skin folk ain't kin folk. We must worry about the ones who want liberation. Harriet Tubman said it best, "I freed a thousand slaves. I could have freed a thousand more if only they knew they were slaves."

The second keynote speaker was Brother Nuri Muhammad. Brother Rizza Islam served as the third speaker. Ta'Juan fell asleep midway through Brother Nuri Muhammad's presentation. Ta'Juan missed out on some gems Nuri Muhammad dropped during his speech. I was curious as to why they have the title "Brother" in front of their names. He soon provided the answer to my curiosity. "The root word of "*brother* is "*other*" Nuri Muhammad declared. As he continued his words of wisdom, a large projector screen began to slowly drop down behind him. "When using the word brother, you are meaning another reflection or extension of yourself. So, if you learn to properly love and respect yourself, then you can do the same for your people."

After Muhammad concluded his remarks, the crowd showed their appreciation with a round of applause, and he took his seat. Rizza Islam was up next. He started with "As-Salaam-Alaikum," and few members of the crowd responding with, "Walaikum-salam". He continued, "I'd to begin with a message from a brother of mine who sadly could not make it. The magnificent Brother Ben X." I remember being on Instagram not too long ago and seeing Brother Ben X talking about some digital real estate course he provides for the people. I still don't know a lot of details about it, but I plan to tap into his stuff soon. Rizza Islam pulled out a paper from a folder and then continued, "The message from Brother Ben reads, *Peace family, my deep apologies for not being in attendance but my schedule is airtight. I wish Brother Rizza and the rest of the speakers the best in their effort to uplift, re-educate, and progress our people. We can first do so by tapping into our God bodies. Take some accountability and initiative to learn our history and wealthy building behaviors on our own. We can't just depend on institutions and programs that have extensive histories of not having the best interests of Black people to properly teach or progress us. If I was to take a picture of the entire setting, the audience would more than likely want to see the picture, because they're in the picture. They would have a lot more interest in the picture since they are in it."* Rizza Islam then put the letter from Brother Ben X on the podium to show he was finished, then began speaking his dialogue. He picked up from what Brother Ben X touched on. About why it is important to have more Black history implemented into our households. Not depending on K-12th grade curriculums offered by white-owned, operated, influenced, or controlled schools. He also said something about the aspects of when a Black child investigates the history books, the school systems provide them, they don't see themselves. Or if they do, it is in a demeaning, inferior, or degrading fashion. If Blacks are also called African American, why is there not just as much Black history implemented into school curriculums as there is white history? Brother Rizza Islam went in on how our last names don't belong to our people, but they belong to our forefather's slave masters. He also touched on how America has a long history of medical experimentation and overall medical malpractice against Black people. Sterilizing Black women after they go into hospitals for minor procedures, using Black people as test rats for dissection and anatomical studies, using science to de-humanize us and throw us in literal circus attractions, the Tuskegee Syphilis experiments, Philadelphia experimenting on Black inmates, Indiana taking woman re-productive rights, and more.

After Brother Rizza ended his speech, the crowd once again applauded with loving approval. Mr. Donley hopped back on the mic, "Alright-alright!" he said overly excitedly. You could feel the happiness on his face. He continued, "We will now tune in to a last-minute special guest! I'm still in disbelief that I was able to connect with her. Once we get these technical difficulties fixed, she will be on the other end of this video call to speak with us." A projector screen dropped slowly down from the ceiling. It came down a few feet behind the speakers. It showed a virtual waiting lobby, indicating us ready to go but now waiting for the person on the other end to join. Twenty seconds later, after connecting a cord from the speakers used for the guest speakers to his laptop, immediately a zoom call populated the projector screen indicating that he was waiting for someone to join the video call. I tried to wake up Rolan, but he was in too deep of a sleep. I checked my phone and saw I had a text from Deja reading, "I hope you enjoy the event!" with a kissing face emoji.

"Can you hear me?" Donley asked through the microphone directed to the person on the other end of the video call. There was a five-second silence. He said it again, "Hey... can you hear me on the other end?" There was finally a response from the other end, "Peace and Black power. I can hear you loud and clear." Soon as her face appeared on the screen, I recognized that it was the one and only Assata Shakur. I knew her voice from an Instagram profile I saw about her from a Tupac fan account. She was Tupac's godmother. I was blown away in shock. Assata Shakur had not been able to come back to America since she fled the country in the 1970s due to white terror, unjust treatment by the US government, and breaking out of prison after being unjustly sentenced. She continued, "It's both a pleasure and delight to be in attendance to such an impactful and revolutionary presentation. Mr. Donley and I are meeting for the first time through a mutual associate, so that is all I need to know about his profound character. The least I could do is give a huge shoutout to him and his efforts to improve the overall quality of life for our people. I hope the ancestors and God guides you into righteousness and keeps you well. Keep striving Black family," she said. "Thank you, Ms. Shakur," Mr. Donely said with an ear-to-ear smile. He then ended the video call and raised the projector screen with the touch of a button. There were volunteers wearing "Be the difference" t-shirts setting up tables close to the exit. One table for each speaker with a name tag indicating whose table belongs to whom.

Up next, was activist and author Michelle Alexander. She discussed her award-winning book called *The New Jim Crow: Mass Incarceration in the Age of Colorblindness.* She spoke in such intricate detail about every racial caste system Black/African people have been subjected to since America's initial conception. Chattel or physical slavery, black codes, Jim Crow, segregation, the crack epidemic, war on drugs, medical experimentation/malpractices, political degradation, social castration, and economic exploitation.

The fifth and final speaker was Rolan. He talked about how we as a people need to stop calling one another niggas. "If a white man calls you a nigga, it would be WWIII" the crowd laughed. After ten seconds of giggles, he picked up where he left off, "We need to begin to speak and label our people with a positive form of address. Our men are brothers, kings, and gods, not niggas. Our glorious and graceful women are queens, goddesses, and sisters, not niggas, bitches, and hoes. We need to circulate and return our Black dollars.

We need to first invest in ourselves, then our people. Change the way we utilize our time. Be careful of the content we are taking in. We need to make the necessary internal changes before we seek any external changes. Your physical, mental, spiritual, emotional, and psychological state should be your main priorities. If you have no morals, no values, or no goals, then you cannot possibly progress in any aspect of your life."

Each speaker dropped real knowledge and cheat codes for life. I nudged Ta'Juan a few more times, but it was no use. He was too deep into his sleep. Rolan wrapped up his speech and headed back to his seat. The crowd, including me, gifted him with a roaring round of applause. My life had changed in a matter of two hours. I wondered why I hadn't learned about this stuff in school. It's crazy how Black people have to go out of their way to learn more about their people, but whites can easily learn about themselves at any school, program, or institution. The end of the program had come. Mr. Donley got on the mic, "Thank you all again for the amazing turnout! I'm sure you will all leave here with something new you learned today. Big thanks to our lovely volunteers who assisted with the stadium and chair set-up. Each speaker has one table in place with products for sale, meet and greet, and more!" he said. The tables were lined up by the entry door. Michelle Alexander to the far left, Nuri Muhammad beside her, Rizza Islam, Dr. Umar Johnson, then Rolan. I had never seen so many smiling Black faces at once. I stayed sitting in my seat to watch out for Ta'Juan since he was still sleeping. There was a long line of spectators waiting by each table anyway. I stayed in my seat to wait until the lines slimmed down. Thirty minutes passed and the handshakes from audience members, purchases, and kind words were exchanged. I finally decided Ta'Juan would be okay by himself, and I got in line to speak to Rolan. There were only two people in front of the line finally cleared, then I noticed Rolan was talking to two men. They weren't in line but rather standing behind the table with him. The man on the left wore a black suit, while the one on the right wore a grey suit. I stayed a distance away, allowing Rolan time to finish his conversation. It looked to be intense. The two men he was talking to looked strikingly familiar, but I couldn't pinpoint how I recognized them. Rolan shook their hands, and they headed towards the exit. He then walked over in my direction. We dapped each other up. I spoke first, "Damn bro, I learned a lot today. Aye, what does knowledge of self mean again? Like what do I have to do?" He responded with a grin then said, "I'm glad you were impacted by today's presentation, brother. I suggest you first work on the way you present yourself. Such as, stop thinking and acting like a nigga. This can be done by first, not calling, or referring to yourself, and other fellow Black people as niggas. Start picking up some Afro-centric and Black-focused books. I have one in my car just for you," Rolan said. I hadn't picked up a book since they forced us to in High School.

I almost forgot to ask Rolan about the two men that looked familiar to me but couldn't remember who they were. "Who were those two guys you were talking to?" Rolan answered, "Ah yeah, that was Mater P and Dave Chapelle. I saw them before the program kicked off but only got to talk to them afterward. They real cool people."

I looked at the empty seat in the gym realizing Rolan was no longer there. I had no idea where he wandered off to. I called and left a text message. No response. "He's probably in the bathroom," Rolan said as we stood in the gym scoping around hoping to see him somewhere. "Yeah, you right. Let's just walk toward the door to see if he pops up," I said. He still was nowhere to be found, so Rolan and I walked out of the gymnasium, strolled through the school's main entrance, and headed to our cars. Hopefully, he's outside somewhere. As we eased out the door, we noticed Ta'Juan off into the distance standing by my car. He shivered as Rolan and I approached. It had to be no more than 40 degrees outside. He was standing by my passenger side door. Rolan was parked to the right of my car. He drove an older model Honda. Ta'Juan was shivering and irritated from the cold weather. "Aye, where y'all niggas been at? It's cold as fuck out here! Been standing here for like ten minutes," he said. I responded, "We didn't even know where you wandered off to. Last thing we knew you were sleeping in the gym." "I went to the bathroom and came back but I didn't see y'all so I tried to call but my phone was dead. Looked around and saw this fine-ass woman. She was walking out, so I followed her and got her number. Was already out here so I knew y'all niggas would be here eventually," Ta'Juan said. Rolan shook his head and responded, "You can't control what a man does. I can only control what I do. I'll be patient with you brother Ta'Juan, but one thing you will not do is continue to call me a nigga," he said to Ta'Juan with all seriousness. I added to "Rolan's conversation. "You our nigg- I mean our brother, so we want the best for you. We are saying this cause' we got love for you bro," I said to him, but he didn't listen. He heard us talking to him, but he didn't care enough to listen.

Chapter Five

Root

In the Spring of April 4, 2002, Ta'Juan was born at St. Methodist hospital. Doctors only gave him a 30% chance of living due to a severe case of asthma. His mother died a day later from complications while giving birth to him. Ta'Juan's grandmother and aunt tried to sue the hospital for medical malpractice. There were several times when they would ask for a nurse due to his mother not feeling well and Ta'Juan's grandmother noticing that her daughter was not acting like herself. The hospital shut down a few years later and still has hundreds of medical malpractice cases still open, mostly the neglect and poor care of Black patients. His father died while his mother was 3 months pregnant. He was a sergeant in the US Army when an IED took out him and thirty other soldiers out while sleeping in their barracks.

After his mother's funeral, Ta'Juan's aunt, the younger still of his mother, took him in with open arms. Her name was Waloma Smith. She lived in an upper-middle-class apartment with two children of her own. A son named Jackson and a daughter named La'Diamond. Along with her husband, Andis. Andis was originally from Jacksonville, Mississippi. He found himself in Indianapolis, Indiana after gaining a full-ride scholarship for track and field at Marian University. He decided to stay after graduating. He ran a successful trucking business and made good money. Waloma worked at a local bookstore. They met while Andis was shopping for books about how to run a successful business. He walked in having no clue what section of the store to look. He locked eyes with Waloma who was stocking books on the shelf by the front entrance. The rest is history. Andis was always known for going above and beyond for his children and made sure his wife Waloma got all the love, support, and affection a Black woman deserves. Andis immediately accepted Ta'Juan like he was his flesh and blood.

Ta'Juan had tremendous struggles and difficulties in the classroom. It originally wasn't due to his behavior, but rather had difficulties when it came to reading, writing, and basic mathematic problems. He would voice his frustrations to his teachers about not understanding the words and letters. His eyes and head would begin to hurt when he tried to do anything that involved reading and writing. To him, the words would always float off the paper. Due to teachers not catering to his needs, he began to act out as a result. On top of that, dealing with not knowing and having the chance to meet his biological mother festered in his mind daily. Nearly every day after school, Ta'Juan would come home to his aunt and Andis with the same answers for his failing grades. "I can't get the words to stay on the paper" or "I keep telling my teachers, but they don't listen to me." One day, Andis had enough and said, "That's it! I'm not gone keep letting this school fail my boy! There is only so much we can do at home. They need to give Ta'Juan more one-on-one time or something!" he said with all the loving and care a man could show for one of his sons. "Your aunt will be going up to your school first thing tomorrow morning to the speaker with your principal and teacher directly. I will do my best to go whenever I get another off day," Andis said. Ta'Juan smiled as big as he could and gave Andis a hug.

That very next day, Andis ended up having to work a last-minute 12-hour 6 A.M.-6 P.M. shift, due to one of his employees getting sick, so Waloma contacted the school that morning to schedule a meeting. They set one for 4 P.M. in Ms. Penders' classroom.

It was the day of the meeting. Waloma was now in Ta'Juan's classroom with his teacher. She tried her best to stay polite, respectful, and calm when dealing with Ta'Juan's teacher, but his teacher made it nearly impossible for her to do so. From the beginning of the meeting, his 2nd-grade teacher, Ms. Pender, showed no type of concern or interest in her job or most importantly Ta'Juan's needs and his aunt's concerns. It was almost as if she didn't want to be bothered with helping one of her students excel. "Good evening Ms. Pender, I'm Ta'Juan's aunt and guardian. I just wanted to ask a few questions about how Ta'Juan is doing in class," she said with a small smile from one corner of her lips. It was a forced smile in an attempt to do her best to stay respectful and polite even after the treatment received so far from Ms. Pender. She was trying her best not to slap Ms. Pender across her white-privileged face. Ms. Pender returned the favor by giving Waloma a half-caring smile from the left side of her lips. No teeth were shown from either one of them. She then responded to Waloma, "Well, Ta'Juan is a model student! He has so much potential, and I love having him in class. I have had no problems with him whatsoever." You lying bitch is what Waloma wanted to say. She knew his teacher was lying right through her crooked, coffee-stained teeth and tart breath. But Waloma kept her cool. "Oh, really? That's strange because Ta'Juan tells me differently. He is saying he's already informed you and his counselor about having difficulties reading and writing. Are you sure he has never brought that to your attention?" she asked again. Her left leg began to shake in frustration. She knew Ms. Pender was lying. Waloma's anger was near its peak, but she was calm and collected with her actions. There was a sudden knock on the door. "Come in," Ms. Pender said as if she would rather be anywhere else in the world. The principal, Mr. Eddison, walked in. He was an older white man with a salt-and-pepper beard. "Good evening, ladies. Can we by chance take this meeting to my office? My apologies how are you today Ms. Waloma?" he asked with genuine care and concern. Waloma could feel his sincere concern, so her response matched his energy. She showed a slight smile, "I'm doing well thank you for asking Mr. Eddison. That is so nice of you, but I would honestly be doing better if I could get some real answers," she said. He responded, "That's completely understandable and you soon will receive what you are here for. If I may, is it okay if we move from Ms. Pender's classroom to my office? I'd like to speak with Ms. Pender for a few seconds so you can take a seat outside for a few," he said. He shot a look at Ms. Pender, indicating his frustration with her. She shot a look of frustration right back at him.

They all got up and traveled down the narrow hallway to Mr. Eddison's office. "Please take a seat right here ma'am. I'll only be a few seconds with Ms. Pender," he said as he assisted Waloma into a chair inside of his office. Waloma responded to his courteousness, "Yes, I would very much like that. Thank you, sir." He exited then shut the door to speak with

Ms. Pender outside of his office. She sat inside his big office and could hear every word he spoke to Ms. Pender as they stood in the hallway. "I can't believe you went against my guidance!" he said firmly and sternly to Ms. Pender. Ms. Pender was supposed to direct Waloma to his office upon arrival instead of to her classroom. He then lowered his voice as if he realized he could be heard by Waloma. After a few more minutes of conversation with Ms. Pender, Mr. Eddison soon entered his office to join Waloma. "I am so sorry about that mix-up," he said as he sat in his chair behind his desk. Waloma was sitting on the other side of his desk. Mr. Eddison had informed Waloma that Ms. Pender would be out of the job in the next week or two after he informed the school board of her lack of communication with the counselors and with him. It wasn't the first time she had done something like this. Mr. Eddison then said, "Today is Friday, so first thing Monday morning I will have a psychologist come in to examine Ta'Juan for any possible mental or psychological issues that could be the factor of his classroom struggles." Waloma was hesitant to approve of such a process being done. She was nervous about what could potentially happen to Ta'Juan in the future if he was to be diagnosed with any mental disorders or a learning deficiency. She was having all kinds of thoughts running through her mind. Will that limit or hold Ta'Juan back from having a normal life? Like what happens if a child is diagnosed with a learning disorder? Does that mean forcing him to take medications? She thanked Mr. Eddison for his time and then left. She never scheduled the evaluation to be done.

Ta'Juan's classmates somehow heard about Ta'Juan possibly having a learning disorder. They made fun of him every day. They would ask him to read or do a simple math problem. Ta'Juan would try his best, but he just couldn't manage to do it. He soon realized how to get his classmates to stop laughing at him and start laughing with him. Ta'Juan started to become the class clown by doing anything foolish to get their laughs and acceptance.

Hard times found their way to Waloma, Ta'Juan, and the entire family. Andis business declined due to having trouble keeping workers. He eventually had to shut down all operations. He found a decent job working as a supervisor at a local medical logistics company, but they let him go after finding out he lied on his application. He had a felony back when he was 19 years old. He also had a really bad drug addiction at this time. He was cool when smoking weed but lacing it with cocaine is what strung him out. It started when a so-called friend of his laced his blunt without him even knowing. He was six years clean until he relapsed. His felony came when he was out clubbing with a friend of his when some guys were harassing a woman he was seeing at the time. He ended up beating one of them up so severely that he almost died. He served two years in jail and one on probation. He was relieved of his job instantly after only a month of work. Andis and Waloma had begun arguing almost every other day due to finances and Andis had re-developed drug addiction. They were now two months behind on their mortgage, lights, and water scheduled to be cut off next week, credit cards maxed out, and one of their two cars got repossessed earlier that morning. "I thought you said you were going to be done with that shit now that we have kids Andis! When did you start using again?" Waloma said to Andis in the middle of the living room. All three of the kids, including Ta'Juan, could hear every word. Andis said nothing in response. Just sat on the edge of the bed watching a Jay-Z music video on BET with a bottle of Hennessy in his hand. He was high as a kite. It was the first time they had had any intense verbal exchange, around their children. Waloma was still talking as Andis grabbed his car keys, grabbed his red Pelle-Pelle coat, walked out of their bedroom, and stormed out of the house. Waloma fell to the floor and cried as soon as the door slammed shut. The kids and Waloma would have never thought that would be the last time they saw him alive.

Hours had gone by and Waloma just knew that something was wrong. Andis had never been gone this long without calling. Local law enforcement called Waloma a day after Andis had left their home. They said that his car was abandoned at a gas station and there were signs of a robbery. Also, signs that Andis was nowhere to be found.

Days, weeks, then months flew by as Waloma and the three children suffered from not having the breadwinner present in the household. She ended up having to pick up a second job as a clerk for a local blood bank. She moved them out of the house with the little money she had left and into a small apartment in the lower-middle-class part of Nap. A small two-bedroom on the east side of the city. Ta'Juan's acting out and rebellion at school grew more intense now that he had no masculine figure to come home to. Waloma was doing her best to support three children on her own. Ta'Juan was the oldest at the time; nine years old, Jackson was eight and La'Diamond was five. They often had to watch themselves while Waloma worked. To make matters worse, Ta'Juan got into some serious trouble at school. He was fighting constantly and was accused of commenting on his teacher's butt, suggesting that her ass was "thicker than a bowl of oatmeal." When asked where he learned it from, he said that he saw it on TV. It was strike three for Ta'Juan at school. If they were truly keeping count, it would probably be strike number one thousand. The school tried to be lenient and understanding due to their circumstances, but this time, they couldn't let it slide. He said something inappropriate to a teacher in front of the entire classroom. Ta'Juan got expelled, giving Waloma no choice but to send him to live with her mother and who was Ta'Juan's grandmother. It was the only way he could get into another school. This didn't stop his behavior inside and outside the classroom. His grandmother was too old to enforce any type of real discipline as a parental figure. Waloma was too financially constrained to visit him frequently since she was struggling to carry two jobs at once. She picked up a third job as a warehouse worker for a local FedEx warehouse. His grandmother was too focused on remembering dates for her doctor's visits, what time and day she needed to take her pills, and making sure she stayed updated on the city bus route changes so she would be at work on time. She worked part-time as a greeter at Walmart.

Now living at his grandmother's house, Ta'Juan called Waloma every day after school. She would answer whenever she was able to due to working so much. He would have called her every minute of the day if he could. He was making friends but still having the same issues at his new school with his new teachers being no help. Waloma always made sure to let Ta'Juan know how special he was. She made sure to let him know that people will always have something to say about you, but it's up to you how you react to them. Ignore them and keep pushing forward. Live your life the way you want. Do whatever makes you happy. You only get one life." She would always ask if he went to church on Sunday with grandma. She'd always ask how he was feeling. She was the first person to show him genuine love. One day, when Ta'Juan tried to call, the phone had been disconnected due to her failure to pay the phone bill. The following weekend, his grandma allowed him to catch the local IndyGo city bus #87 to visit her. Waloma welcomed Ta'Juan into her apartment with open arms. Jackson and La'Diamond were glad to see him as well. The three of them played outside all day until it was time for Ta'Jaun to go back home. His grandma was cooking dinner at six o'clock, so he needed to be home by five, so he could clean up and shower before dinner. He said goodbye to his cousins and then ran inside the apartment to give Waloma a big hug before his bus ride back to his grandmothers. Waloma smiled as she hugged him tightly. She began to cry. "Why you crying, auntie? I'll be back to see you," Ta'Juan said. She wiped her tears. "I know baby. I'll have a special surprise for you when you visit us again," she said. He walked out of the small apartment, optimistic for the next weekend so he could ride the city bus back over to Waloma's apartment. It normally is a twenty-minute bus ride from Waloma's apartment to his grandmother's home, but traffic caused a forty-minute bus ride.

As soon as Ta'Juan got off the bus to his grandmothers', he saw cops had surrounded the place. There was a yellow tap around her yard. An on-duty officer could be heard yelling, "stop that little boy," as Ta'Juan forced his way through the crowd of officers to look for his grandmother inside. When he finally made his way in, he noticed his grandmother looked a lot lighter than normal. She always tells him to never lie on the floor, so he was confused about why she was on the floor laid out. She looked as if she was just taking a really good nap. The officers surrounding her were doing as much as they could to bring her back to life as they waited for the paramedics to arrive. None of the officers on the inside noticed that Ta'Juan was standing at the front door viewing it all. "How long until the fucking ambulance gets here?" one of the officers yelled with full force, but it was no use. His grandmother was gone. It wasn't until one of the officers from outside the house ran in after Ta'Juan. Ta'Juan stood at the front door with a blank facial expression. He couldn't comprehend what exactly was going on. The cop who ran in from outside tapped Ta'Juan on the shoulder and then bent over to speak to him. "Hey, little man. What's your name?" Ta'Juan turned around from the cop and sprinted out of the house. Two cops tried to chase after him, but he outran the cops enough to where they lost sight of him. He was on his way to the city bus stop. He immediately caught the next #87 bus to head back to Waloma's apartment.

After a twenty-minute bus ride, he arrived at the bus stop that was down the street from Waloma's apartment, which would be as close as he could get. A large crowd hindered him from getting any closer. The apartment was engulfed in flames. The dark smoke could be seen from miles away. As the fire grew more out of control, fire trucks were on the scene doing what they do best. Police had the whole block secured. No one in unless you were a paramedic or a firefighter. One of the neighbors peeped Ta'Juan standing by himself. His two cousins spotted him too. Waloma's neighbor had his cousins with her as she approached Ta'Juan. "Come with me baby," she said in a way older Black grandmas do. They were headed to the police station. As they all piled into the neighbor's car, La'Diamond and Jackson didn't even look in Ta'Juan's direction. They said nothing to him the entire car ride to the police station.

There are laws in place that don't allow minors to be interviewed without a parent or guardian, but Ta'Juan had neither. So, the cops pulled some tricks to be able to question him about the fire. They were suspicious since he had a history of bad behavior and was the last to see Waloma alive. His cousins told the cops that Ta'Juan had left Waloma's apartment just minutes before they began to see the smoke. They were playing outside when they saw him running out of the apartment. Everyone thought that Ta'Juan had intentionally set his own auntie's apartment on fire. Even his cousins. Accused of killing the woman who brought him in and opened her heart to him. Ta'Juan was hurt because he would never do anything to intentionally harm her. It took months for forensic reports to come back, declaring that Ta'Juan was innocent. It was a faulty wire in the stove which sparked the initial flames, but the damage had already been done with the relationship of Ta'Juan with La'Diamond and Jackson. It later also came out that his grandmother died from a heart attack after receiving a phone call from the police that Waloma was killed in a house fire. Losing both of your daughters would be hard for anybody to live through. A young boy never being able to meet his biological parents, then accused of killing the woman he saw as a mother figure, then seeing his grandmother lying dead in her living room. You can only imagine the psychological and emotional tole all of this took on Ta'Juan. There was no other family for Ta'Juan, Jackson, and La'Diamond, so they wound up in foster care. A good middle-class family ended up adopting Jackson and La'Diamond but passed on Ta'Juan due to his track record. Ta'Juan would live the rest of his years of youth in foster care. He hasn't seen or heard from Jackson or La'Diamond since. The only reason he was allowed to stay at his current school was because his counselor, whom he saw twice a week as part of his foster care service, recommended it was best for him to stay in close contact with his friends. The only loved ones and support system he has left.

Chapter Six

Loving

Deja and I talked every day, between us both working and her going to school. We'd talk on the phone almost every night but mostly talked through text. Some nights I wouldn't be able to call her due to working the night shift at a second job I picked up as customer service for an insurance company. I love working at Vicks, but the paychecks aren't holding me over too well. I make $900 every two weeks at Vicks. My rent is $1,200 alone plus groceries, gas, and other essentials I'm left with no money to save. With my part-time customer service job, I get to work from home, but that is the only perk when dealing with rude customers over the phone all night. Cussing at me, lying when we have proof of what happened, I've heard it all. One night, an older lady tried calling me saying she was never involved in a type of car accident. I looked up her case file. I explained to her that there is an entire police report, including surveillance video of her running two red lights and causing a three-car pileup. The street cameras didn't just catch her license plate number, but also snapped a picture of her in the driver's seat driving the car. That didn't stop her from still denying and lying about having any involvement.

Friday came. I was originally scheduled to work 11 A.M.-6 P.M. but Rey asked me to come in at 10 A.M. at Vicks to help him display the new all-red Nike Air Force ones and take inventory. He handed me a twenty-dollar bill for coming in an hour early. I made it to my lunch break when I decided to grab a quick burger. I made my way to the food court. While in route, I pulled out my phone from my pocket and called off my second job. I just needed a break, man. As I was heading to the food court, I passed by Victoria's Secret without pausing, but I did a quick peep inside. I was a few steps past the store when I circled back to see if Deja was at work. I walked in examining the different lingerie, leggings, and other feminine clothing and attire. I eventually saw her behind the register, folding clothes and talking to somebody through her employee headset. She didn't see me walk in, so I calmly walked up to the register. "Wassup Deja. How's work going so far?" I asked. She finally popped her head up from the folding. She smiled brightly like she always does. "It's going great now that you're here. You on break?" she asked, happy to see me but wondering what I was doing. I responded, "Yeah, when do you take your lunch break?" I asked. She responded, "Whenever I want since I'm the manager. Why who's asking?" she said, blushing as she swung her arms back and forth. I shared her excitement. She didn't know what I had planned but she knew it was something that would involve us spending quality time with each other. I laughed and then responded, "You are funny. Let's go check out that new arcade they put in the mall." She lit up like a Christmas tree. She had this magnificent sparkle in her eyes. I'd see it anytime she was excited about something. "Okay, give me two seconds," she said. She took off her headset, ran over to one of her employees who was hanging up a few jackets, and whispered something to her. I'm not sure what she said, but they both seemed happy and excited. They shot each other a look filled with joy. No words just a shared joy. She ran back over to me and said, "Okay let's go."

I was excited about the arcade for a few different reasons. Number 1, I love playing any type of video game. I had an X-Box when I was younger but now, I have a PlayStation 5. Secondly, I get to spend time with Deja. It had been a while since we were able to hang out since I'd been working so much. Lastly, it was cheap. I had just paid rent and finally got my car speakers fixed, so I checked my bank account on my phone as we walked out of Victoria's Secret. My mobile banking app indicated that I had $352.63 in my account. The entrance to the arcade had no doors, just an open entry. A small black machine sat to the left as soon as you walked in. It had big orange letters on it reading "5 tokens per $1!" There were no employees on site. Only multiple gaming stations. Atari, Pacman, Mortal Kombat, an ice hockey table, and more. There were some games that I had never even seen before. I pulled out the twenty-dollar bill I had in my wallet. I put twenty in the machine for 100 gaming tokens. Something was wrong with the machine because it began to shoot the tokens out faster than we expected. We giggled and had the time of our life as we scrambled to grab the tokens shooting at us with hostility. "Don't let them hit the ground!" I said to Deja as a friendly challenge. We didn't let a single token hit the ground. After hustling to ensure we had all of our tokens, Deja bosted out, "Ooh a Pac-Man game!" and took off in a full-on sprint. I speed-walked behind her. When I got there, she took one leap into the air filled with excitement. Her eyes lit up brighter than the colorful flashing lights of the gaming stations. "I used to play Pac-Man all the time with my dad. It was a special father-daughter thing we did together!" she said. She looked so stunning and gracious in everything she did. I told her about my thoughts on how she looked like I always do. This time instead of blushing, she just looked into my eyes as if she was trying to see if I meant what I said. We stood there staring at each other for about twenty seconds. Time seemed to pause for us. The only noise came from the sound effects from the different gaming stations. I pulled her closer to me and dove into her deep, darkened lips. Her lips complemented her skin to pure perfection. That one kiss seemed to last an eternity. Having her in my arms felt better than anything I've ever experienced in my life.

We played a few more games. Pinball twice, then basketball, which had a two-minute timer to see who can make the most shots, a sit-down race car game, and at least ten rounds of table hockey. I kept beating her, and she didn't want to leave without at least one win. She never got the win she was striving for. After she finally accepted defeat, it was time to head back to work. I was twenty-five minutes past my break, but I didn't care. Rey wouldn't trip because it was slow today. I walked her back to her store. I said that I would Facetime her later tonight. She said that she would be waiting for my call.

I was back at work. Two things were on my mind. How perfect Deja is and quitting the customer service job. The money is good, but the hours are terrible. 8 P.M.-1 A.M. is too much, especially after working a day shift at Vicks. I just feel like there is something else calling for my time, energy, and effort. Not a bullshit customer service job. Like I could be spending my time more efficiently doing something else. Rolan was calling me, so I answered, "Aye wassup bro," I said. He responded, "As-Salaam-Alaikum brother, have you checked the group chat?" referring to the group chat with Rolan, Ta'Juan, and me. I hadn't been on my phone since before I linked up with Deja. "Nah I haven't checked my phone in about three hours," I said. Rolan chuckled and said, "You might want to check it out. I think Ta'Juan is not so hardheaded after all." Then Rolan hung up as quickly as he had called.

It got a little busy at Vick's, so it took about thirty minutes until I had some downtime to check out what Rolan was talking about. Customers were coming in asking about shoe releases, prices, and inventory. When it finally slowed down at work, I pulled out my phone to check the group chat. I couldn't believe it. I was so shocked that I didn't just think to myself, I had commented out loud, "Oh shit." Ta'Juan was asking about what books he should buy to gain more self-knowledge. He also asked if we wanted to go to church with him this coming Sunday. I passed but thanked him and said how proud I was that he was starting his self-exploration journey. Rolan thanked him for the offer but reminded Ta'Juan that he was a Muslim. Muslims go to the mosque or masjid for prayer, like how Christians go to church. I got off work at 8 P.M. then I drove home. I took a shower and Facetimed Deja until around 11 P.M., then I fell asleep after we talked for about an hour.

Chapter Seven

Dreamer

I had a dream about Deja that night. Sometimes I can't remember my dreams clearly when I wake up, but I can remember this one as clearly as day. It started with me driving. I was on my way to pick up Deja. Ta'Juan helped me earlier to clean my car out since he was the main reason for all the random trash in my car. Every time he rides with me, he leaves trash between the passenger seat and the door instead of throwing it away. I had brand new air fresheners too; Black-Ice scent. My dad always had that scent in his car. It's one of the many things I picked up from him. Also, a man should never walk with his hands in his pockets. A man can ask for help but never take a handout. A man doesn't let his emotions control his actions or cloud his judgment. A man provides and protects in all aspects. Another influence Pops has on me is music: Gucci Mane, Rick Ross, Lil' Wayne, Bun B, Pimp C, Kanye West, Boosie, Webbie, OJ da Juiceman, chopped and screwed tracks, and more. I put him on my generation's music, but there are only a few artists he likes. He listens to Kendrick Lamar, Lil Baby, Future, J Cole, and Drake. Took him a while to come around, but Pops also listens to Young Thug now.

This is the part of my dream when I finally met up with Deja. I texted her, "2 minutes away." She texted back, "okay," with a heart emoji. It was during winter because there was light snow descending from the sky. I was wearing a fresh black Nike jacket, black fitted jeans, with black and white Nike Dunks. I finally pulled up to our apartment. We were living together. She walked out with an extra hoodie in her left hand and her purse in her right hand. The hoodie she was wearing read "Goddess" in gold trim on top of the continent of Africa on her chest. She must have gotten it from the Black-owned clothing store AKQ (Aboriginal Kings and Queens). She also wore black ripped jeans and black Timberland boots. She handed me a black hoodie that she surprised me with and wanted me to wear. It had a picture of Malcolm X's mug shot on the chest, along with a quote underneath it:

"It is important for you and me to spend time today learning something about the past so that we can better understand the present, analyze it, and then do something about it."

- Malcolm X

I threw my Nike jacket in the back seat of my car and put the Malcolm X hoodie on. She had a few snowflakes in her hair from the light, snowy weather. She's one of those girls that like to do romantic stuff, like dress in coordinating outfits. I don't mind it at all though. I was just enjoying being in her presence. Being able to experience this one life we have together.

We finally pulled off and headed towards the location Deja put into the GPS on my phone. I had no idea where we were headed. I just knew that it was fifteen minutes away, based on Google Maps. Another reason this was a good dream is because I was driving a Benz Truck. My dream car. I normally drive a little recklessly, but I drove cautiously with Deja riding with me. I'd sometimes merge into lanes with no turn signal and speed up when I see a yellow light instead of gradually slowing down, but all that was out the window with Deja riding with me. She is precious cargo. The songs in rotation ranged from Erykah Badu, Summer Walker, Janet Jackson, Jill Scott, Rhianna, Beyoncé, Musiq, Miguel, Jodeci, Tony! Toni! Tone!, Maxwell, and The Isley Brothers.

We finally pulled up to a skating rink parking lot. I could tell by the big neon sign on the outside that read Skate City. Deja knows damn well I don't know how to skate. She laughed and said, "I'm going to show you how to skate baby. Don't worry. I'm surprised one of your little girlfriends hasn't taught you yet." We both laughed. I responded, "What makes you think I have other women around?" She looks me right in the eyes and says, "I know you used to get around Joel. I'm not stupid. Don't play with me Joel," she said. I laughed it off and then got out of the car. I shut my door and then jogged over to her side of the car to open her door for her. You would have thought I had just given her one million dollars the way she lit up from me opening her door. She held onto my right arm as we walked into the skating rink. It was jam-packed as always for a Saturday night. Probably because it was free entry for couples and only two dollars for skates. Her eyes watered with emotion as she said, "Thanks for taking me out with you tonight, Joel. You make me feel so special."

It was around 9 P.M. when we got there. After about five steps from the entrance, we immediately made a left to rent out some skates. "Size 5 please," she said. I then said my size, "Let me get a 10 bro." I attempted to pay for both of our skates, but she insisted that she pay for us, so I let her. We went off to the side next to the concessions to a brown bench to sit down and put on our skates. I could already see other couples having the time of their life out on the skating rink. A few were falling flat on their butts, then laughing it off as they recuperated. Others were falling forward, barely having enough time to catch themselves with their hands to avoid making first contact with their faces. The DJ was going crazy in the music booth. The booth stood above; ten feet tall in the middle of the skating rink as skaters dashed around in a huge circle. The music selection was impeccable. He played all the hot artists, such as G-Herbo, Lil Uzi, GloRilla, Megan the Stallion, and more. Deja liked rap music, but she loved R&B even more. She was vibing religiously to every song that was played from the bass-filled speakers.

Deja had put her skates on in a matter of seconds. It took me a while due to being so nervous. I became more collected once I stood up, took a few steps, and started to get the hang of it. Plus, Deja held on to me the entire night, so that was my biggest help. She was teaching me the basics. Keep one foot in front of the other, don't be so tense, and stop looking down. I was comfortable enough to let her show me a few tricks. A light inside of a circular colorful ball hung from the ceiling. It spun around in circles, creating a reflection of colored lights filling up the entire rink.

The lights seemed to be magnifying Deja's distinctive beauties. It felt good knowing that I had the most magnificent woman in the building. After a handful of rap songs, my favorite songs by Michael Jackson came on, "Lady of my life," "Butterflies," and "Got to be there." Deja and I both knew the songs by heart. I found out that night that she is a huge Michael Jackson fan, just like me. She's always been full of surprises. This dream was almost too good to be true. I had become a decent enough skater now, to the point where I could dance a little while skating. That's how I knew I was dreaming because I never dance. It's almost as if the whole world went mute in our favor. All my senses were fixated on Deja. I could tell she was feeling the same way. A true soul connection. Mind, body, and spirit. A soul attraction. We held each other as we lapped around the rink. Michael Jackson's voice seemed to be everlasting. I felt as if he had made that song just for me and my goddess. One thing about dreams while they're happening is that they seem so real. I was having the time of my life. "Ah shit, look at my nigga Joel going crazy on the floor! I see you, bro! I need to get like you!" the DJ said over the microphone. The entire rink caught wind of what the DJ was saying and soon, they all directed their undivided attention to Deja and me. I soon noticed it was my nigga Deshaun that was DJ'ing that night. He also worked at Hot 96.7 radio station during the daytime. I soon realized we were the only two on the skating floor. Everyone else was outside the rink recording us on their phones, eyeing us in awe, wishing in their minds to one day find a unique connection like ours.

After we exited the rink, we sat at a table near the concessions. I read Deja's body language and could tell she wanted to take a break. From what I have heard, they have okay food, for a low price. I like the sound of cheap. Deja was rocking to a throwback jam Deshaun was playing. Tevin Campbell "Can We Talk." I bought Deja a slice of cheese pizza and a pink lemonade from the drinking fountain. She doesn't like pork and doesn't like ice in her drinks. Ta'Juan, surprisingly, pulled up with some random girl I have never seen before. I didn't ask any questions about it. The two of them sat by us. "Y'all look like y'all having more fun than anybody else in here," Ta'Juan said. "Yeah, this is one of the best nights of my life," Deja said in response to Ta'Juan as she looked deep into my eyes. It felt good knowing that my date in my dream with Deja was going perfectly.

I asked Ta'Juan to take a picture of the two of us. I handed him my phone. "Make sure it's on portrait mode," Deja said as Ta'Juan got into a photographer's position. The pics came out better than I thought. Damn near looked like a professional photographer had taken them. Deja posted the best picture, in her opinion, out of the twenty pics Ta'Juan took. I thought I looked weird in all of them, but Deja implied that I look good, so I said, "fuck it." She quickly posted them on her Instagram, TikTok, Twitter, and Facebook. If MySpace was still around, she would have posted it there as well. The caption read: "Date night with my man" with a brown heart emoji she loves to use when referring to me. She tagged me, so I immediately got the notification on my phone. I went to her profile and liked our pic she posted on her Instagram. I also shared it on my Instagram story. "That's all you're going to do Joel?" Deja said jokingly. "What you talking about goddess?" I said, laughing, and a bit confused. "Why can't you comment on your queen's post on social media?" she said jokingly. "Because the whole city already knows that you're not my queen. You my goddess," I said, as I dove into kiss her warm thick brown coated lips. I never felt so good in my life. I felt right with her in this wrongful, cruel world. I never had a dream this powerful before. I wanted so badly for it to be real.

Some guy ended up falling on the skating rink floor hard enough to sprain his ankle. A few people helped him off to the side, away from the rest of the skaters. "Ah shit, somebody call this nigga an ambulance," Deshaun said over the microphone as he lowered the volume of the skating rink music. "Nigga hell nah!" that man who rolled his ankle yelled in response, hoping everyone at the rink heard. "You know how much an ambulance cost? Nigga call me an Uber. They can take me to the hospital."

Chapter Eight

Folks

I spent an entire Sunday and Monday reading through the three books Rolan gave me. The Autobiography of Malcolm X, The Miseducation of the Negro by Carter G. Woodson, and the first three chapters of The New Jim Crow by Michelle Alexander. My entire world was ruptured. I felt like I had been taught wrong my entire life after being exposed to the true realities and history of Black life. I never knew what real racism is. I thought it was over and done with. It happened a long time ago but now everything is good. I learned that racism is not just mere words that make you feel a certain way. It's not always right in your face. Racism, true racism, comes with power. The power to hold a group of people captive for 300 plus years, strip them of their names, language, freedoms, and overall being of themselves. After erasing everything about their history and culture, then letting them go "free" while one particular group of people benefits from an entire empire built from the backs of free Black labor. Also, enying people access to basic life essentials and their due reparations. The CIA, FBI, and other American government entities have begun vilifying, demonizing, criminalizing, or even killing pivotal Black activists who were simply striving to truly free their people from white supremacy then later years praise them as heroic human beings to push off accountability. Malcolm X, Martin Luther King, Assata Shakur, Nina Simone, Angela Davis, Fannie Lou Hammer,

Fred Hampton, Medgar Evers, and the list goes on. The FBI opened cases against all of them. Think about how hard it is for a group of people to fight back after seeing so many of their people receive cruel sometimes lethal backlash for their opposition against white domination. I also read a few things about racism and slave-like teachings in religion. For example, in my grandmother's house and many churches across America, there are pictures of Jesus depicted as a white man. Some people say he is white, even though there is overwhelming evidence proving he was of color. Why does he have Caucasian features, such as long brown hair and blue eyes, in almost every picture of him at churches, cathedrals, and many other places of worship when the Bible says he has heard like wool and skin like bronze? Why was Jesus freshly lined up with a goatee every time I see a white fake picture of him? They didn't even have barbershops back then so how did he get a line up? Christians, Muslims, or even people with no religious preference would have to agree that he was a Black man. You can even take all religious aspects out of this conversation and use common sense to figure that out. I see it as clear and blatant racism that has been implemented into the minds of the masses with white folks being at the top. White folks thought if they lied and tell us Jesus was white then that must mean God is white. This implies that white people must be the superior race if God is a white man.

There is no coincidence that there is one American holiday deemed worthy of celebration each month. Christmas in December, Thanksgiving in November, St. Patrick's Day, Valentine's Day, and the list goes on. The history behind these holidays is evil and often anti-Black. Why must you celebrate pagan holidays to show you love, care, and cherish somebody? Spending your last for gifts you can't even afford to further support the white economic power structure? You are late on your rent but buying chocolate, flowers, and a plus-size teddy bear to prove you love your wife. Buying your family over-priced shoes for Christmas but have a major car issue that hasn't been fixed yet. Buying turkeys on Thanksgiving when Thanksgiving is about pilgrims or white individuals persecuting and slaughtering masses of Native Americas while Africans were enslaved during this holiday's initial creation. Christmas is not mentioned in the bible not once. It stems from an old Roman holiday called Saturnalia where men would rape, become overly intoxicated, kill, and more. The 4th of July is nothing but a celebration of white domination. The Declaration of Independence was signed at a time when Black people were considered property, not people. So, who was the Declaration of Independence referring to when it stated freedom and liberty to all people? The American government and international white power structure used religion, sports, politics, economics, and more to keep Black people subjugated and divided.

Black people are the most faithful voters in America. We always encourage each other to vote, and we need representation in political offices, but we still have no actual power. We've been in political seats for over a century now. Black women and men are in seats of office across the nation, but no tangible or concrete gains have been made for our people. They have done their best for the Black masses, but it is a difficult stride to bring justice to your people when the foundation of a country was built upon your suffering. America's government has given us tokenism for years instead of true freedom, justice, and the pursuit of happiness. Malcolm X exposed all of their tactics and agendas during his life on this earth along with many other pivotal Black revolutionaries. Democratic and Republican party members are notorious for giving Black people fancy rhetoric, articulations, symbolism, and sophisticated metaphors instead of real-life gains as a people.

Chapter Nine

Elevation

Ta'Juan has been consistent with his new lifestyle. I pulled up to his apartment so we could talk in my car. He was going at it with his baby momma again, so we just chilled in my car. I had Nipsey Hussle's Victory Lap album playing. It was 10 A.M. so I just wore the yellow Adidas hoodie with the decal on my left chest, some grey sweatpants I got from Walmart, and black crocs. He texted me earlier and said he wanted to talk about a few things that have been on his mind. "I had a dream a few days ago," Ta'Juan said. "My aunt Waloma was in my apartment standing in the kitchen washing my dishes. She dried them off while saying how much she loved me and that she knew the fire that killed her wasn't my fault," he said as he took two hits and then passed me the blunt. He let out three coughs after the second hit. I took a hit, looked at it a little cause' it was really hitting, took another then passed it back to him. Then he continued, "She also was telling more about how she has such high hopes for me. She said I have so much to give, but I just have to work to find myself first. I think what Rolan been talking about will lead me to the point," he said as he passed me the blunt. I took a hit from the blunt. I decided to quit my second job. It just wasn't worth my time anymore. Ta'Juan started to talk about some new book he just got. "Aye, Rolan put me on a book by Dr. Amos Wilson. I bought it off Amazon a few days ago. It's called The Falsification of Afrikan Consciousness. I'm curious to know why he spelled Afrikan with a 'k' instead of a 'c,'" he said. I was both proud and excited that my brother was finally elevating and progressing.

After we got done talking, Ta'Juan and I rode out. He needed a ride to his cousin's house for God knows what. I didn't ask for details. He asked for a ride, so I'm just looking out. Ta'Juan was sitting in the passenger seat and with my phone hooked up to the aux. He started playing a new Babyface Ray album. My phone started to ring as I got on the highway. The default iPhone call ringtone raved through my car speakers. Ta'Juan turned the music down. "Aye bro, Deja calling," he said. I forgot I was supposed to call Deja when I woke up this morning. She said that she had an important exam at school today, so I was planning to surprise her with a call for support and encouragement. I answered the phone. She was excited. "Baby, I passed my exams! Like I really thought I would do bad, but I killed that shit!" she said. I was so proud of her. Her energy always had a way of rubbing off on me. Even through the phone, I felt her love. I matched her energy, "I'm proud of you baby! I knew you would be ight. You've been studying night and day. It was just a matter of time before all of that hard work would pay off." Ta'Juan was in the passenger seat laughing and whispered to himself, "Cake ass nigga," he said under his breath. I ignored Ta'Juan and continued my conversation with Deja as if he was not there. She asked me what I was doing tonight. "I'm picking you up tonight," I answered. I didn't have to be in her physical presence to tell that she was blushing through the phone. "Okay, baby. See you later," she giggled.

I hung up the phone and laid it in my cup holder. Ta'Juan asked me an interesting question. "Do you think Deja is going to be here for the long run? Or are y'all just fucking?" he said. "I'm not sure but we ain't even fucked yet bro," I responded. I never realized that I haven't even had sex with Deja until Ta'Juan brought it up. Deja is the first of so many girls I have been with that sex didn't cross my mind. It's more than just a physical attraction when it comes to her. Her beauty is not only physical. Her personality, determination, intelligence, aspirations, and kindness are most beautiful to me. She had a plan. Most people our age can't say that. She pushes me to do better and to elevate myself as well. Especially when we talk about what I've learned from the books I've been reading.

It was around 3 P.M. when we pulled up to his cousin's spot. "Ight bro I'll catch you later," Ta'Juan said as he extended his arm out. "Ight bro. Be safe," I said as I dapped him up. He stepped out and shut my door. He took three steps towards his cousin's house, then paused, turned around, and faced me. He signaled to roll my window down. I did. "Wassup bro?" I asked confused. He dug in his pocket and tossed a knot of money tightened with a rubber band onto the passenger seat. "Hold that brotha. It ain't gas money for the ride either. It's just an appreciation gift. Be safe bro. Imma' text you later." Then he headed up the driveway to his cousin's front door. I paused for a few seconds to stare at the money as it lay still on my passenger seat. I can only imagine how he got that money, but I needed it and appreciated him. I rolled my window up and pulled off.

I wanted to get Deja's favorite snack before I picked her up; watermelon sour patches. She also likes my Black-Ice air freshener, which hangs on my mirror, so I got a new one. I brought the items up to the register. I didn't pay too much attention to the cashier as I walked. When I got to the counter, I laid my two items at the counter waiting for a purchase. I was looking down at my phone until I heard the cashier speak to me. "Is this all for you today bro?" the cashier said. I finally looked up, and I noticed it was D'Marcus behind the checkout register. I had no idea he worked here. "Ah shit, wassup bro. My fault I didn't notice when you walked in. I was busy counting the register. I'll finally be off work in fifteen minutes," D'Marcus said. He looked tired from a long day of work. "It's all good bro," I dapped him up. "How long have you been working here?" I asked. "About a month. The costs for my school went up this year. My momma can't work anymore. Her boss said that her frequent days of absence due to doctor visits and sickness is not good for the company. I told her she should sue they ass," D'Marcus said as he rang up my items. I handed him a $10 bill. He gave me back my change along with my receipt. "They think...," D'Marcus' voice got low, and he started to look down at his hands, "she might have cancer bro." My heart sunk into my chest. I did notice the last time I saw her; she looked like she had lost a lot of weight. Much smaller than I remember. I thought she had just been working out recently. With his mom out of work, he had to pay not only for his high school but also be the man of the house and pay most of the bills. "Gotta see if they'll at least give her unemployment until we figure everything out," he said as he grabbed a plastic bag to put my items in. He then handed them to me. I knew that he was in a tight spot. I talked to him for the rest of his shift and walked him to his car. Before he drove off, I told him that hard times don't always last. I didn't know what to say but wanted to still let him know I was there to help in any way I could.

I texted Deja, "Ten minutes away." She recently moved out of her parent's house. They retired from their jobs and bought a house in Florida. She wanted to stay in Nap for school, so she found an apartment of her own. She hadn't texted me back by the time I got to her apartment. I was now sitting in my car outside of her crib waiting for her to text me back or call. Fifteen minutes had passed. I was about to pull off when I finally got a call from her. "You can just walk in baby. I'm apartment number 17B. First floor," she said. I was excited to see the inside of her apartment. I grabbed the snack I got for her, turned my car off, and walked up the sidewalk to her apartment. As I knocked on her front door, it creepily opened. Unlocked, so I walked in. "Aye Deja, it's Joel. You need to make sure your door is locked. Anybody could have walked in," I told her. I locked the door behind me. I sat her candy on her red velvet couch. "I'll be out in a second," I heard her yell from somewhere in her apartment. Her living room carpet rested only a few feet in front of the couch. They both shared the same color which looked to have red-velvet ocean wave patterns on them. She didn't have a TV in the living room, which wasn't surprising since she's a book reader. Where people normally put a TV a few feet across from the couch, she had a small bookshelf. Her mini library consisted of two rows of books. I got a closer look. I recognized a few of them. If Beale Street Could Talk by James Baldwin, The Coldest Winter Ever and Midnight from the Sister Souljah series, Becoming by Michelle Obama, and A Wasteful Love which was the movie we went to go see not too long ago. A few names from the spine of the other books were familiar. Angela Davis, Toni Morrison, Yaa Gyasi, Maya Angelou, and Alice Walker. She had one huge painting that seemed to be plastered over every inch of one of her wall. From a distance, it seemed to focus on love and happiness. I went closer for a better examination. It was a massive 40x40 creative beauty. It was of a Black body without a face or hair. Had two arms and legs but no hands. Two legs and feet but no shoes. She wore a long, wide, grey oversized T-shirt that drooped to her ankles. Streaks of warm heart-filled colors surrounded the straight-standing Black body. Shades of red, yellow, and orange were all over. I was in for a surprise when I saw the signature on the bottom right corner. "Deja N.," short for Deja Noles. She never told me painting was a hidden talent of hers. "Aye Deja, you never told me about your artwork. This is dope for real! How long did it take you...?" Before I could finish Deja appeared from the back to the living room area. She stopped and posed two feet away from me. A great silence suffocated the room. The only noise that could be heard was her heater blowing heated air. Her right arm leaned on the wall allowing her sweet body to lean against the wall. She pushed her left hip out. She wore tight revealing clothing that exposed sites of her I had never seen before. Her skin and hips were smooth and refined. The body oil she was wearing magnified her already radiant skin. Her skimpy red track shorts and a white tank top with no bra allowed me to see her pretty nipple piercing on both nipples. Her shorts were tight enough to limit her front putting a piece of paper in her pocket. A great portion of her butt hung out the bottom half of her shorts. Every visible part of her body showed more of her distinctive treasures. She took a few steps closer. We stood face to face. Her delicate hands grabbed the chest area of my shirt pulling me even closer toward her. My manhood stiffened as my craving to ease inside her flower intensified. With her being a few inches shorter than me, my face slightly leaned down toward hers. She looked up slightly at me with her graceful brown stained eyes. She was still gripping my shirt when I began declining my hand from her coke bottle waist and stopping at her soft and firm butt pulling her even closer. We began to kiss each other with a slow passion. Her left hand was now caringly massaging the outside of my pants where my dick was wide awake. I put my left hand to her chin to move her head upward. I began to smother her neck with passionate kisses. She let out a moan that got me even more ready to make love to her. After two minutes of neck-kissing, I went back to her lips. Her short arms then swallowed around my neck as we continued the meeting of our lips. My left hand was already on her ass, so I took my free right hand to meet it. I pressured both hands against her to pick her up. Her were arms still around my neck and our lips were still joined together. She had a one-bedroom apartment, so it was easy to find her bed. I laid her down with ease and tender care. I kissed all over her heaven-sent body. She smelled amazing. Her skin was softer than a silk scarf. Her hair was tied up, so we didn't have to worry about it getting in the way of anything. I posted my right hand on her neck and applied a gentle degree of pressure. She didn't move my hand or indicate she didn't like it, so I continued. While gripping her neck, I began to lick and caress her left nipple. I dropped my right hand to her pussy. It was warm and drenched with excitement. The building anticipation drew out more intense moans from both of us.

Chapter Ten

Liberation

My mouth transitioned from her breasts, a few slow passionate kisses to her stomach, then to her flower. I teased her with a few kisses on her vaginal lips before my tongue stimulated her clitoris. I used my ring and middle finger to further please her. Her hands rested on my head. She continued to squirm and moan as I continued to deliver what seemed to her an unbearable sensation. Her body began to quiver. Her moans grew louder. My dick grew harder. She reached her first climax faster than I expected, to be honest. I continued to give her oral pleasure until she was wet enough to my liking. I began to kiss upward. Her wetness was all over my lips and chin. She was ready. I began to kiss upward. Her nipples were firm and pointed. Her body began to talk to me. I stood up, pulled down the waistband of my sweatpants, and pulled out my manhood. Her eyes instantly locked on to it. She played with my dick with her feet. I used my left hand to post up her right leg. I hunched over slightly and entered. She was warm and welcoming. She gasped. We both began to moan as I slowly stroked in and out of her world. My manhood was growing stiffer while I was inside of her. Her body shook intensely with pleasure. Her face twisted as if she was holding back tears. I dropped her leg and laid over her. Her nails dug slightly into my back. I flipped her over to her side. We spent ten minutes going at it in that position. The sweat from my forehead had dripped onto my nose. We both reached ecstasy. She then kindly pushed me off and buried her face into one of her four soft pillows. She assumed the position. Her ass swayed left and right in the air. I knew what she was asking for. I went back to work. She enjoyed the way I drilled her from the back. Her hair was in my dominant right hand as I pulled back gently. We spent twenty more passionate minutes making love.

We ended up falling asleep. I was lying on my back with Deja's face on my chest. I woke up to Deja playing with the few hairs I had on my chin. Hopefully, one day I'll be able to grow a full beard. "Your phone was ringing. I tried to wake you up, but you were knocked out," she said, still playing with my few chin hairs. She reached over to a small nightstand she had on her side of the bed to grab my phone. She then handed it to me. When I looked, I had a text from both Rolan in our group chat. Rolan had sent a link suggesting a video for us to watch by Dr. Claude Anderson. I put my phone down. Deja got off my chest and walked to the bathroom connected to the inside of her bed. She cut the light on. She then turned on a portable speaker that sat on her sink. She came back to the bed to grab her phone under a pillow. I gave her a kiss on her forehead. She smiled and returned to the bathroom. She looked down at her phone and shuffled through to pick out a song. She looked back at me laying on the bed, "You okay with listening to Solange? I always like to put her albums on shuffle," she asked. "Whatever you want baby," I responded. The interlude: Tina Taught Me by Solange played. I sat listening and became lost in staring at her ceiling. Then it hit me. I had it all figured out.